# FRIENDSHIP IS TESTED IN CABIN SIX

KATIE always had good ideas, but as play director she was just plain bossy.

SARAH was very proud of the play she had written and very hurt by Katie's changes in her script.

MEGAN's patience was pushed to the limit by Katie's constant yelling.

TRINA usually played the peacemaker, but Katie's bossiness was too much even for her.

ERIN was pretty happy but only so long as she was playing the glamorous leading role.

MARILYN KAYE is the author of many popular books for young readers, including the "Out of This World" series and the "Sisters" books. She is an associate professor at St. John's University and lives in Brooklyn, New York.

Camp Sunnyside is the camp Marilyn Kaye wishes that she had gone to every summer when she was a kid.

# Katie Steals the Show

## Marilyn Kaye

AN AVON CAMELOT BOOK

CAMP SUNNYSIDE FRIENDS #6: KATIE STEALS THE SHOW is
an original publication of Avon Books. This work has never before
appeared in book form.

AVON BOOKS
A division of
The Hearst Corporation
105 Madison Avenue
New York, New York 10016

Copyright © 1990 by Marilyn Kaye
Published by arrangement with the author
Library of Congress Catalog Card Number: 89-91531
ISBN: 0-380-75910-1
RL: 5.2

First Avon Camelot Printing: March 1990

CAMELOT TRADEMARK REG. U.S. PAT. OFF. AND IN OTHER COUNTRIES, MARCA
REGISTRADA, HECHO EN U.S.A.

Printed in the U.S.A.

OPM 10 9 8 7 6 5 4 3 2

For Alan and Robert Burstein

# Katie Steals the Show

# Chapter 1

Katie Dillon was feeling restless. It had been raining all day, a steady drizzle that looked like it would never end. She glared out a window in cabin six and mentally ordered the rain to stop. But she knew that even with all her confidence and authority, she just didn't have that kind of power.

Except for running to the dining hall for breakfast and lunch, the cabin six girls had been inside all day. Rain meant no horseback riding, no swimming, no archery. Of course, there were indoor things to do at Camp Sunnyside on rainy days. Right this moment, at the activities hall, games and organized activities were going on. There was probably lots of action over in the arts and crafts cabin, too. And movies were being shown in the dining hall.

But in cabin six, the girls were just hanging

1

around. Katie felt like she was in jail. She couldn't understand why none of the others seemed to feel that way. From her perch on her upper bunk, she surveyed them.

On the top bunk across from her, Sarah Fine was reading. That meant she was perfectly content. Given a choice, Sarah would probably spend every day, even the sunniest ones, right here inside the cabin with a book.

Across the room, on her single bed, Erin Chapman was experimenting with Megan Lindsay's hair. She was trying, without much success, to force Megan's red curls into a French braid. Katie watched as Erin tugged and yanked at Megan's hair. It looked painful to Katie, but Megan offered no complaint. On closer observation, Katie could see why. Megan's face had that familiar glazed expression which meant she was off on one of her usual daydreams.

Katie leaned down over the side of her bed and peered at the bunk beneath her. Trina Sandburg sat cross-legged on her bed. She held a piece of cloth bound by a hoop. It looked like some sort of embroidery. Katie watched for a minute while Trina patiently made little knots and stitches. It looked boring.

Well, she wasn't doing any good for any of

them just sitting here feeling restless. She had to get this gang going.

"Hey, guys, let's go over to the activities hall. There must be something happening over there."

"Are you crazy?" Erin asked. "It's still raining. Do you have any idea what this weather does to my hair? I still haven't recovered from the frizz I got at lunch."

Only Erin would put her hair before fun, Katie thought. "What about you, Megan?"

"Huh?" Megan responded dreamily.

"Megan's not going anywhere," Erin stated. "I've almost got this right."

Katie leaned down over the side again. "Trina? Want to go to the activities hall?"

Trina looked up. "I guess I could," she said slowly, "if you really want to." But Katie could hear the reluctance in her voice. She knew Trina was only agreeing to please her.

"Sarah? How about you?" She knew the question was hopeless even as she asked it. And Sarah's response was exactly as she expected. She shook her head, her eyes not even leaving the page of her book. "I'm just getting to a good part."

Katie fell back on her bed and groaned. Usually, she could rouse the group to follow her suggestions. She'd always prided herself on her ability to get her cabin mates to follow her lead. This was all very annoying.

From her private bedroom, their counselor, Carolyn, emerged. "Well, you guys are certainly quiet today."

"It's this darned rain," Katie said.

"Hey, no excuses are necessary," Carolyn said, smiling. "I'm not complaining about the quiet. It makes a nice change." She sat down on Megan's empty bed. "What's this Sunnyside Spectacular I keep hearing about?"

"It's just a dumb show," Erin said, still tugging at Megan's curls. She must have pulled unusually hard because Megan actually came out of her dreamy state.

"It's not so dumb," she said. "Sometimes it's fun."

Katie scrambled down from her bunk and joined Carolyn on Megan's bed. Obviously, it was up to her to explain to their first-year counselor what the Spectacular was all about.

"It's like a variety show. A whole cabin can do something or you can perform by yourself or whatever. We invite other camps in the area to see it."

"What kinds of things do people do?" Carolyn asked.

Trina looked up from her embroidery. "Last

4

year, this girl did a ballet dance. She was really good."

Sarah put her book down. "And *we* had to go after her, remember? It was humiliating!"

"Really? What did you guys do?"

"We sang," Katie told her. "We took some rock songs that were really popular, and Sarah put new words to them so they all had to do with Sunnyside."

"That sounds cute," Carolyn said.

"It was *awful,*" Erin replied.

"It wasn't that bad," Katie protested. Since it had been her idea, she felt like she had to defend it.

"It was a good idea," Trina assured her. "And Sarah wrote some really funny stuff. The problem was, none of us can sing."

Erin raised her eyebrows. *"I* can sing."

"Yeah," Sarah said, "but the rest of us drowned you out. We were so out of tune, no one could tell what songs we were imitating."

"And I forgot the words." Megan sighed.

Sarah summed up the experience. "It was a total disaster."

Katie was about to object to that description, but she couldn't. Sarah was right. It was a disaster. And even though no one in the cabin blamed her, Katie couldn't help feeling it had

5

been her fault. She shuddered as she recalled the titters and giggles of the audience. That wasn't going to happen this year. Not if she could help it.

Carolyn smiled sympathetically. "So what are you doing this year?"

Silence fell over the room. Katie didn't have to look around to know that all eyes were on her. She'd always been the one who determined how they'd participate in the Spectacular. And now they were all waiting. Waiting for her to come up with a brilliant idea, a fabulous scheme. The Sunnyside Spectacular was on her shoulders.

And for the first time in the three years they'd all been coming to camp, she didn't have the slightest notion as to what they were going to do.

"Remember our first year?" Trina asked. "We put on sort of a circus show. Megan and I were acrobats. Sarah and Erin wore lion costumes, and Katie was the animal trainer."

"That sounds like fun," Carolyn said. "Couldn't you all do something like that again?"

Erin made a face. "I hated that costume. It itched."

Katie considered the idea. "We could do something *like* that. Maybe we could be clowns . . ."

6

"Forget it," Erin said flatly. "Didn't you hear Ms. Winkle say we're inviting Camp Eagle this year to watch it? I'm not going to be a silly clown in front of boys."

"Besides," Sarah added, "I think we should do something more original."

Katie had to agree. Too many kids at camp would remember their circus show. They didn't want to repeat themselves.

"Cabin nine is having a fashion show," Erin reported. "Megan, hold still." Now that she was out of her fantasy world, Megan had started fidgeting.

"Gross," Katie said. "We can't do anything like that."

"No kidding," Erin said. "I can't even get Megan's hair to look halfway decent."

"Give up," Megan said cheerfully. She ran her fingers through her tight braid, and all her unruly curls popped out.

"What about a folk dance?" Trina suggested. "Like that one we learned last year."

Katie hesitated. "I don't know . . . I mean, that might not be the best thing for all of us . . ."

"It's okay," came Sarah's voice above her. "You can say it." She climbed down and joined Carolyn and Katie. "I've got two left feet. When we were learning those folk dances, I was tripping all over my feet. And everyone else's."

"I don't want us to do anything people are going to laugh at," Erin said.

"Why don't you all go over to the activities hall," Carolyn suggested. "You could hear about what some of the other kids are doing. That might spark your imagination."

"Actually, that's a good idea," Trina said, putting her embroidery down.

"Yeah, I'm getting tired of lying around," Sarah agreed.

Even Erin got up. "I'm going to have to wash my hair later anyway. I might as well let it frizz."

Katie's mouth dropped open. Just a few minutes ago she'd been pleading with them to go there. Now, just because Carolyn suggested it, they were ready to go. She was on the verge of pointing this out to them, but suddenly they were all grabbing their hooded raincoats. Feeling just a little disgruntled, she got her own.

It was good to be out, even in the rain. They all ran across the camp to the activities hall. Since there wasn't much else to do at camp on a rainy day, the place was packed. Ping-Pong balls flew back and forth across tables. A bunch of the younger campers were gathered on the

8

floor around a counselor who was telling stories. Other campers were sitting at card tables playing board games.

"Let's find out what the kids in cabin seven are doing," Trina said. They headed toward a corner of the room where a bunch of girls were sprawled on the floor putting together a gigantic jigsaw puzzle. It was the kind with zillions of tiny pieces that all look alike.

"Hi," one of the cabin seven girls called. "Come help us out."

Katie picked up a piece and tried one space, then another. Casually, she asked, "What are you guys doing for the Spectacular?"

The cabin seven girls exchanged glances. Katie read the looks they were giving one another.

"We're not going to copy you," she said indignantly. "We just want to make sure no one's doing what we're doing."

One of them relented. "It's going to be neat. We're imitating rock stars. Like, one of us is going to be Madonna, and another one's going to be Cyndi Lauper. *I'm* dressing up as Michael Jackson."

"And we're going to play their records and lip-synch the words," another girl informed them. "That's not what you're doing, is it?"

"Oh, no," Katie assured them. "Ours is much different."

"What a fantastic idea," Megan gushed. "I wish we'd thought of it." Katie shot her a dirty look.

But later that day, over dinner in the dining hall, Katie found herself wishing the same thing. Erin would have made a fantastic Madonna.

She looked around the noisy room. At every table, girls were talking. Was it her imagination or did they seem more excited than usual? They're probably all planning their acts, she thought glumly.

"Have you guys come up with an idea for the Spectacular?" Carolyn asked them.

"No," Trina said.

"But we will," Katie added quickly, with a lot more confidence than she was really feeling. Frantically, she searched her mind for an idea. She had to come up with something. Her reputation was at stake!

"What about a magic show?" she proposed.

Carolyn looked at her with interest. "Can you guys do magic tricks?"

"Well, no," Katie admitted. "But there are these kits you can buy that teach you how. My brothers had one once . . ." Her voice trailed off. Except for Trina's expression of polite interest, there was a total lack of enthusiasm on the group's faces.

"Of course, we don't have to come up with our own idea," Trina said. "There's no rule that cabins have to do Spectacular together. We can even split up and do something with other cabins."

"But we've always done our own thing," Katie protested.

"That's fine too," Trina said quickly. "But what's our own thing going to be?"

Katie was still pondering the dilemma as the girls started out of the dining hall. Georgina from cabin nine crossed their path and paused.

"Hi, Erin, I was looking for you. Listen, do you want to be in our fashion show for the Spectacular?"

Erin hesitated, and Katie broke in. "We've got our own plans."

"Okay," Georgina said. "See you later."

Erin turned to Katie in annoyance. "She was asking me, not you. You could have let me answer."

"You weren't going to say yes, were you?"

Erin shrugged. "Well, if we don't come up with anything—"

"We will," Katie said firmly. "Besides, you don't really want to get involved with those cabin nine girls again, do you?"

She gave Erin a meaningful look. The last time Erin had tried hanging around with those older girls, she'd gotten herself in a mess of trouble. They were always doing illegal things, like sneaking across the lake to Camp Eagle or hitchhiking into Pine Ridge, the closest town. All the cabin six girls had had to band together to get Erin out of what could have been a serious jam.

"No, I guess not," Erin said reluctantly. "But you'd better come up with something good for us to do."

But as much as Katie racked her brains, nothing came to her. All evening, she thought and thought, but her mind was a blank.

"Thought of anything yet?" Megan asked her as they were getting ready for bed that night. And much to her embarrassment, Katie had to admit she hadn't.

She could almost feel the reproachful looks being sent her way. Silently, the girls got into their beds. And then Sarah's soft voice pierced the silence.

"I've got an idea."

Everyone sat up. "What is it?" Erin asked.

"We could put on a play."

Katie stared at her across the room. "What kind of play?"

"An original one."

Katie rolled her eyes. "And just where are we going to find an original play?"

Sarah reached under her mattress and pulled out a notebook. "Right here." An abashed smile crossed her face. "I wrote one."

# Chapter 2

"You wrote a *play?*" Trina sounded positively awed. "When?"

"I've been working on it a long time," Sarah said. "Sometimes during free period or whenever I could get out of doing something else. Anyway, I finished it last week."

"You didn't tell me about this," Megan remarked with mild reproach.

"I didn't tell anyone. I wasn't sure if it was any good. But I read it over this morning. And now I think maybe it's okay. And I've been thinking, maybe we can put it on for the Spectacular."

"It's not a romantic play, is it?" Katie asked apprehensively. She remembered when Sarah was hooked on reading romances.

"No. It's more dramatic."

Katie still had doubts. "But—a whole play? For the Spectacular?"

"Why not?" Trina asked.

"Because . . . because I've never seen any group do a whole play at Spectacular. Maybe a funny skit or something, but not a whole play."

"But that's what makes it a neat idea," Trina said. "It's something different and original."

Carolyn's door opened, and the counselor stuck her head out. "Lights out, girls."

"Carolyn, Sarah wrote a play!" Megan announced. "And we're going to do it for Spectacular!"

Carolyn came out of her room. "What's the play about, Sarah?"

"It's called 'The Search for Happiness.' It's about how the Spirit of Happiness is kidnapped by the Spirit of Meanness. So all the people are really sad and depressed all the time. These two groups go out looking for her. One group is smart, and the other group is strong. But they can't work together because the Spirit of Meanness is ruling them. Once they get close to the Spirit of Happiness, she sends out good feelings, and they figure out how to cooperate so they can free her."

"Wow!" Megan exclaimed. "That's really neat!"

"I'm very impressed, Sarah," Carolyn said. "What do the rest of you think?"

"It sounds like a good story," Katie admitted. "But how many parts are in it?"

"Six," Sarah said. "The two spirits, the two smart people, and the two strong people."

"Then how can we put it on?" Katie asked. "There are only five of us."

"I've got an idea," Carolyn said. "I was talking to Laura, the counselor in cabin five. She told me they don't have a project for the Spectacular yet. Why don't you invite them to join us?"

Erin looked appalled. "Cabin five? They're only ten years old!"

That wasn't bothering Katie. After all, the younger kids didn't try to take over and run things. But something else occurred to her. "But they've got six girls in cabin five. That'll make eleven of us. Now there's too many girls and not enough parts in the play."

"But everyone doesn't actually have to be in the play," Carolyn told her. "You'll need someone in charge of props, someone to paint the scenery—"

"Oh, good." Trina sighed in relief. "Can I have one of those jobs? I get terrible stage fright."

"And you'll need a director, too," Carolyn

continued. "Someone to take charge of everything and tell everyone what to do."

Katie was pleased to see that all eyes had turned to her. "That's what I want to do. I'll be the director, okay?"

There didn't seem to be any objections to that. And loyal Trina immediately said, "You'd be perfect, Katie."

"Good grief, look at the time," Carolyn said. "You guys are supposed to be asleep. We'll talk more about this in the morning. And I'll talk to Laura and see if the cabin five girls want to go in with us on this."

"I'll want to have a meeting of the whole group tomorrow," Katie said. "Sarah, I'm going to make this play the best event of the whole Spectacular!"

"I'm sure you'll all work together to do that," Carolyn said. "Good night, girls."

Katie settled back under her covers and smiled happily. Okay, maybe the Spectacular project wasn't her idea. But at least she'd be directing it. And she could make sure this show wouldn't be a disaster.

Cabin six was unusually crowded the next afternoon during free period. There were all the usual inhabitants, plus the six girls from cabin five and their counselor, Laura. As soon as everyone was settled on beds or the floor, Katie took charge.

"We're going to be putting on a play that Sarah wrote for the Sunnyside Spectacular. It's called 'The Search for Happiness.' "

"Is it a fairy tale?" one of the cabin five girls asked.

"Oh, no, nothing like that," Katie said. "It's more like an adventure." But the girl's comment struck her. With a title like "The Search for Happiness," it did sound sort of like a cutesy-poo fairy tale. And a Camp Sunnyside audience would turn their noses up at that.

"Sarah," she said, "can we change the title? How about 'The Battle of the Spirits'?"

Sarah didn't look very pleased with that. "You don't like my title?"

"Oh, it's a very nice title," Katie said quickly. "But it sounds a little"—she tried to think of a nice way to put it, but she couldn't—"a little wimpy."

Now Sarah looked positively offended. Trina jumped in. "I think what Katie means is that it sounds, well, not very exciting. And the play is so exciting, you want to have a title that shows that."

"I think 'The Battle of the Spirits' sounds better," Megan said. "More dramatic."

"Oh, all right," Sarah said. Katie rewarded

her with a big smile. She hoped she hadn't hurt Sarah's feelings. But it was for the good of the play—and that's what had to come first.

She turned back to the others. "Okay, it's called 'The Battle of the Spirits.' Anyway, do you cabin five kids want to do it with us?"

There was a general bobbing of heads among the younger girls, and they all looked pretty interested. There was one exception, though—a pretty, dark-haired girl who just looked bored.

"I guess the first thing I should do is give out the parts," Katie continued.

"Uh, Katie," Trina said, "some of us don't know each other. Maybe we could introduce ourselves first."

It was good advice. Katie herself wasn't sure she knew all the cabin five girls' names. And she ought to at least know the names before she gave out the parts. "Okay," she said. "I'm Katie and I'm the director." The other cabin six girls introduced themselves.

Then the cabin five girls began. "I'm Fran," said a cute girl with very short fair hair. She had a high squeaky voice that made her seem even younger than she was.

The skinny one with long bangs hanging into her eyes spoke softly. "My name is Karen."

The identical pigtailed twins were Jill and Jenny. And a cheerful-looking, freckle-faced girl

**19**

was named Becky. The girl with the sullen expression mumbled something.

"What?" Katie asked. "I couldn't hear you."

The girl looked at her in annoyance. "Dinah. My name is Dinah."

Katie couldn't help noticing the looks the other cabin five girls gave one another. Obviously, Dinah was not one of the more popular girls in their cabin. "All right, we know each other's names," she said. "Now, I'm going to give out the parts."

"What's the play about, anyway?" Becky asked.

Here was a chance for Katie to make up for any hurt feelings Sarah might still be harboring. "Sarah, why don't you read the play out loud?"

Sarah was taken aback. "The whole thing?"

"It's not that long," Katie said. "And I want everyone to hear what a great play it is, so they'll all get really excited."

Sarah blushed slightly. "Well, okay." She picked up her notebook.

"Act one. Sandy, Mandy, Gina, and Tina are playing together. On the other side of the stage, the Spirit of Happiness is pointing a wand at them. Gina: Isn't this fun? Sandy: Yes, we always have fun together. Tina: It's nice that we always have good times together and never fight. Mandy: That's because we have the Spirit of Happiness with us. Spirit of Happiness: And I will always be with you to keep you happy and joyful and friends forever."

As she went on, Katie found herself totally caught up in the tale. She hadn't just been flattering Sarah. It really was an exciting story. When the Spirit of Meanness entered and captured the Spirit of Happiness, it was so dramatic that Katie actually felt shivers.

The other girls seemed completely absorbed in the story too. Even Dinah was looking mildly interested.

Sarah read with a lot of expression. Katie could actually visualize the girls bickering and yelling at each other as they attempted to rescue the happiness spirit. And she found herself breathing a sigh of relief when the Spirit of Happiness got the girls to cooperate so they could free her from the mean spirit.

"Did you really write that all by yourself?" Karen asked.

Sarah nodded. And everyone looked impressed.

"I want to be the Spirit of Happiness," Erin said. "She's the star, right? I could wear a crown, and a silk dress . . ." Katie could tell she was already seeing herself looking glamorous

21

and beautiful. And she didn't miss the narrow-eyed look Dinah gave Erin.

"Have you ever been in a play before?" Dinah asked her.

"No, but the part's perfect for me," Erin replied complacently.

"I want to be one of the strong girls," Jill cried out. "Look!" She flexed her arm and pointed to a tiny muscle.

"Me, too!" Jenny yelled, and made an identical muscle.

"You can't both be on the same side," Megan argued. "No one will be able to tell you apart."

"I want to be meanness," Fran squeaked.

"Can I just work on scenery?" Karen asked. "I don't want to be onstage."

It seemed like everyone in the room was talking at once. Katie clapped her hands together briskly. "Hey, shut up!" Nothing happened. She looked at Carolyn and Laura helplessly.

"Girls," Laura called out, "listen to Katie." They quieted down, and Katie shot Laura a grateful look. But she hoped that in the future she wasn't going to have to depend on counselors to get the girls to pay attention. Counselors usually weren't involved in planning Spectacular programs. It was a Sunnyside tradition for the campers to do this on their own.

"Look, I have to think this over before I decide who's going to get which part," she told them.

Erin frowned. "But what if you give us parts we don't want?"

Katie hadn't considered this. Once more, she turned to the counselors for help. "Katie, why don't you hold auditions?" Carolyn asked.

"Huh?"

"Let each girl try out for the part she wants."

It was a good idea. Katie wished she'd thought of it first. "Okay," she said. "We'll have auditions tomorrow. We'll all meet in the dining hall during free period."

"How do you do an audition?" Jill asked.

Katie wasn't sure. And she was forced once again to turn to the counselors.

"You could read from the play," Carolyn suggested. "I'll take Sarah's copy over to Ms. Winkle's right now and get it duplicated. Anyone who wants to try out for a part can take a copy and study the part tonight."

"And it's just about time for dinner," Laura said. "So let's go back to our cabin, girls."

The meeting split up, and the cabin five girls followed their counselor out. The cabin six girls busied themselves washing up and getting ready for dinner. While all the others were in the bathroom, Megan came over to Katie. "Are

23

you really going to let Erin be the Spirit of Happiness?"

"I don't know yet," Katie said. "She sort of looks right for the part, in a fairy-princess way. But she doesn't much act like a spirit of happiness."

"That's what I think, too," Megan said. "Erin can be awfully snotty sometimes. So I wanted to ask you if *I* could be the Spirit of Happiness."

Katie looked at her in surprise. "You?" Somehow she couldn't picture Megan, with her mischievous face and red curls in that role.

Megan nodded eagerly. "It's so romantic!" Her eyes went all soft and dreamy. "I want to wave the wand and make everyone happy."

Katie considered this. Megan was definitely a cheerful person, and when she wasn't daydreaming, she was bubbly and exuberant. But there was a problem. She hated to bring it up, but it was important.

"Megan, do you think you could learn the part? There are a lot of lines. Remember how you forgot the words when we did that singing show?"

"Oh, Katie, I'd practice so hard. I know I could memorize them if I really tried." Her expression was so earnest that Katie could almost believe her.

"Well, maybe. I'll see."

Megan grinned, and hurried off to wash her hands. Katie thought about it. She'd certainly rather give Megan the starring role than Erin. Not that she disliked Erin, but Erin would undoubtedly let the role go to her head. She'd start *acting* like a star—even more than she already did. And one thing she knew for sure—Megan would definitely take Katie's directions better than Erin would.

But Megan would have to do a good audition, Katie thought as she left with the others and started toward the dining hall. If she didn't, Katie couldn't take a chance on letting her ruin the play. She was thinking about the other girls and the other parts when she realized Carolyn was walking beside her, while the others were way ahead.

"I was looking for a chance to talk to you alone," Carolyn said. "You know, I've been involved in theater work at college. And I just wanted to give you some advice."

"About what?" Katie asked.

"Tomorrow, at the auditions ... be careful, Katie. It's easy to say exactly what you think without considering people's feelings. If two girls try out for the same part, only one can get it. And you want to try very hard not to hurt the other person."

"But I have to make sure the right person gets the right part. Isn't that the director's job?"

"Absolutely," Carolyn agreed. "But just be tactful, okay?"

Honestly, Katie thought, what did Carolyn think she was going to say to someone—you stink? "I will," she assured the counselor. And she promised herself she would try not to get anyone upset or angry.

But only one person could get each part. And it was Katie's job to make sure it was the best person. As much as she didn't want to hurt anyone's feelings, the success of the play was the most important thing.

She could only hope everyone else would agree.

# Chapter 3

The girls were clutching copies of Sarah's script as they gathered in the dining hall the next day during free period. Several of them looked nervous as they pored over pages, moving their lips as they silently practiced. Every now and then they'd glance up at Katie with awkward little smiles.

Observing them, Katie was glad to see them looking worried. It meant they realized how important this was. But it made her nervous too. She had a big responsibility. At this very moment, the success or failure of this play was on her shoulders. Everything depended on her making the right decisions.

Chairs had been pulled away from the tables to form a semicircle in front of the stage, and the girls were sitting there. Carolyn and Laura were in the dining hall too, but they'd taken seats farther back at a table. They didn't seem to have any intention of interfering. Katie alone stood in front of the chairs.

She clapped her hands sharply. "Can I have everyone's attention?" She was pleased to see that this time everybody responded. They fell silent, sat up straight, and looked at her expectantly.

"Let's start with the Spirit of Happiness," Katie said. "Who wants to try out first?"

Megan's hand shot up.

"Okay, Megan. Go on up to the stage."

Megan went pale. "In front of everyone?"

"Of course! That's where the play's going to be. You better get used to it."

Megan giggled. "Oh, right." She rose from her chair, climbed the stairs to the stage, and stood in the middle. "Um, what should I do?"

Katie tried not to let her exasperation show. "You're supposed to read some of the spirit's lines."

Megan looked at the script in her hand. "Which ones?"

Katie flipped through her own copy. "Read the scene on page five, when the mean spirit arrives."

"Okay." Megan located the section, coughed, and began.

It was probably one of the most dramatic

scenes in the play. But you'd never know that from the way Megan read it, Katie thought. She stumbled over the words, and she read them with no expression at all. Every now and then, when she mispronounced a word, a giggle escaped her lips.

Katie tried to remain expressionless, but it wasn't easy. What was she going to do? she thought in dismay. Megan wanted this part so much. And Katie wanted her to get it. Maybe with lots of practice and rehearsal . . . but deep in her heart she knew that all the rehearsals in the world weren't going to turn Megan into a proper Spirit of Happiness.

Finally, Megan finished, and came back down. "Thanks," Katie said. From the corner of her eye, she could see Sarah with her arms folded across her chest, shaking her head and frowning. And Katie couldn't blame her. But *she* was the director, and she was the one who had to tell Megan.

"Who wants to go next?" she asked the group.

Erin got up and walked confidently up to the stage. She smiled brightly at the audience, opened her script, and began reading the same lines Megan had read.

Even though she'd just heard them, the words sounded entirely different to Katie. " 'Be gone, evil creature,' " Erin read fervently " 'This is no place for the likes of you. You have no business here!'" As she continued, Katie found herself becoming impressed. Erin was good. Her voice was clear, smooth, and full of feeling. Katie didn't know what a happy spirit should sound like, but she had a feeling this was it.

Erin finished, and left the stage. "Thanks," Katie said, still trying not to let her reaction show. "Now, who wants to try out for the mean spirit?"

"Wait a minute." The sullen-faced girl from cabin five, Dinah, got up. "I want to try out for happiness."

It was impossible this time to keep her reaction from showing. *"You* do?" If there was anyone in the room who looked the opposite of a happy spirit, it was Dinah.

The girl glared at Katie through narrowed eyes. "I've had acting lessons." With that, she marched up to the stage.

She did the same scene the other two had. But she didn't read from the script. She had actually memorized the lines. And once again, it was completely different. " 'Remove your horrid presence from this joyful place! How dare you intrude on our happiness?' "

Talk about expression. Dinah's voice was passionate, angry, powerful. Katie furtively glanced at the others. Their eyes were fixed on Dinah, and they all seemed captivated.

It's a real performance, Katie thought in amazement. But it bothered her. As exciting as Dinah sounded, she didn't come across as a happy spirit. And then Katie had an inspiration. Dinah would make a perfect mean spirit!

Of course, she still had to give the others the opportunity to try out for that part. Fran, the cute fair-haired girl from cabin five, auditioned. She gave it her best, but her high-pitched voice and sweet face just didn't make the part convincing. After much shoving from her twin, Jenny went up on the stage next. She was better than Fran. At least she sounded tough and strong. But she wasn't as good as Dinah could be in the role.

"Who else wants to try out?" Katie asked the group.

"I want to be in the play," Becky said, "but I don't care which part I get."

"Same here," Jill said.

"You still have to read," Katie told them. "Then I can tell which part you're right for."

Becky went first. She read well, calmly and evenly, and Katie made a mental note to put her on the smart team. Jill, like her sister, was lively and athletic looking, so Katie figured she'd be good on the strong team.

"Can I be in charge of scenery?" Karen asked. "I did the scenery for a play we put on at school last year."

"Fine," Katie said. And Trina volunteered to handle the props.

"Sarah, what do you want to do?" Katie asked.

"I figured I could be your assistant," Sarah replied. "After all, I know the play better than anyone. I could help coach the actors."

That wasn't a bad idea, Katie thought. If the others didn't work hard enough or started fooling around, she'd have Sarah to back her up. After all, Sarah wrote the play. She wouldn't want the audience laughing at it any more than Katie would.

"So who's going to play which part?" Megan asked.

"I have to think it over," Katie told her. "Let's meet in cabin six after dinner, and I'll announce my decisions."

The group split up. Cabin five had arts and crafts, and cabin six had horseback riding. As they headed toward the stables, Trina walked with Katie.

"You look worried," she said.

"I am," Katie admitted. "You know, Megan really wants to be the Spirit of Happiness."

32

Trina nodded slowly. "Katie . . . I don't think she can handle a part that big."

"I know that," Katie said. "But—she's going to be really upset if I don't give it to her. And if Erin gets the part, she's going to start acting all stuck-up and conceited."

"You have to put personal feelings aside and think about what's best for the play," Trina remarked.

"I *know,*" Katie said sharply. Then she sighed. "I'm sorry. I guess I'm just a little nervous. Remember last year? I don't want us flopping like that again."

"That's not totally your responsibility," Trina said. "We all have to do well."

"But I'm the one who's going to be telling you all what to do and how to do it. If I give the Spirit of Happiness part to Erin, do you think I can make her do what I tell her to?"

"Well, you're the director. She *has* to listen to you." Trina smiled sympathetically. "You can handle it, Katie."

Katie nodded. Trina was right. She could handle it. And she wouldn't let feelings get in the way. Not hers—or anyone else's.

Once again, the girls from both cabins were gathered in cabin six. The counselors were at a meeting, so it was just the campers this time.

33

And they were all looking at Katie. The last time she remembered feeling this important was when she captained a team in the camp's color war. That had been a big responsibility, too. But this was different. In the color war, the campers knew who was the best runner, the best jumper, the best gymnast. And no one had griped when Katie assigned them to different events. Would they accept her decisions now, too?

"I've decided who's going to play each part," she began. She decided to get the worst part over with first. Avoiding Megan's eyes, she said, "The Spirit of Happiness will be played by Erin."

Erin smiled and nodded, as if this was exactly what she expected to hear. Katie forced herself to glance at Megan to see how she was taking this. Even though she was determined not to let personal feelings interfere with her direction, she was relieved to see that Megan didn't look particularly devastated.

"Congratulations, Erin," she said. "You'll be better than I would have been anyway. I don't think I could have ever learned all those lines."

But someone else didn't seem quite as content with her decision. Dinah looked stunned. Then her expression turned to anger.

Katie spoke quickly. She wanted to let Dinah know she was still getting a good part. "And the

Spirit of Meanness will be played by Dinah."
She waited for Dinah's expression to change. It
didn't.

"I didn't audition for that part."

"But it's a big part, as big as the other spirit,"
Katie said. "And you just seem right for it." The
minute the words left her mouth, she knew it
was the wrong thing to say. It sounded as if she
was telling Dinah she was mean herself.

Dinah stood up, her eyes blazing. "If I can't
have the part I auditioned for, I don't want to
be in this play at all." With that, she stormed
out of the cabin.

"Don't let her bother you," Jill advised. "She
always throws a fit if she doesn't get her way."

But Katie wanted her for that part. She'd be
perfect. "I'll be right back," she told the others,
and ran out of the cabin. "Dinah! Wait up!"

The girl paused and allowed Katie to catch up
with her. Katie spoke rapidly. "Listen, Dinah, I
know you wanted the other part. But this is a
great part, too. And think of the play! Don't you
want to be a part of the Spectacular?"

"I'll be glad to be a part of the Spectacular,"
Dinah said, "if I can have the part I want."

"Well, you can't always get what you want,"
Katie said. "Where's your Sunnyside spirit?
You're going to miss out on all the fun! And
besides, we need you!"

Dinah gave her a sidelong look. "If you need me, then let me be the Spirit of Happiness."

"But you'd be better in the other part."

Dinah sneered. "Then forget it. I don't want to have anything to do with your dumb old play." She stalked off toward her cabin.

Katie gave up. As she went back to cabin six, she tried to figure out who could play the part.

"She's not going to be in the play," she told the others. "So I'm giving the Spirit of Meanness to Jenny."

"Yay!" Jenny exclaimed. "I'll be really mean, I promise."

"Yeah, it comes naturally to her," Jill added. Jenny grabbed a pillow and hit her twin on the head. Jill returned fire.

"Hey, you guys, I'm not finished!" Katie yelled. "Megan, you'll be Sandy, and Jill will be Mandy, on the strong team. Fran and Becky will be Gina and Tina on the smart team."

They all seemed pleased with their parts, and everyone started talking at once. Katie had to raise her voice to be heard over them. "We'll be having the first rehearsal tomorrow."

Sarah edged over to her. "Maybe you should tell them to start learning their lines."

"I was just about to say that," Katie said. "Listen, everyone, start learning your lines, okay?"

She wasn't sure if they heard her. But that was okay. Tomorrow, at the first rehearsal, she'd make sure they all realized how important this was. And, like Trina said, they'd *have* to listen. Even without Dinah, Katie was going to make this play the very best act in the Spectacular.

# Chapter 4

At the pool the next morning, the campers had free swim. Katie always loved free swim days, when they didn't have to participate in lessons. The girls could do anything they wanted in the pool. They didn't even have to go into the water if they didn't want to. The older girls, like the ones in cabin nine, used the time to lie on the pool landing and work on their tans.

Usually, Katie organized swimming relays with her cabin mates, practiced her diving, or just generally horsed around in the water with the others.

Not this time, though. She decided to take advantage of the free time to study Sarah's script. She positioned herself on the landing as far as possible from the cabin nine girls and way back against the gate to avoid any splashing that might get the script wet.

But it was hard to concentrate on reading. The noise from the pool was distracting. The other cabin six girls had gotten their hands on a beach ball, and were attempting a wet volleyball game. There was more yelling and cheering than usual, and all the girls seemed to be enjoying themselves. It looked like a lot of fun. Katie couldn't help wishing she was in the pool with them.

Carolyn had joined them that day for a swim. She climbed out of the pool and came over to Katie. "Aren't you going in at all?"

Katie held the script away from the dripping counselor. "I have to go over the script. We've got our first rehearsal this afternoon. I figure I'd better know this play really well if I'm going to direct it."

Carolyn sat down next to her. "I heard you did a great job of casting yesterday. Everyone seems to be happy about the parts they got."

"Except for Dinah from cabin five. I wanted her to be the mean spirit. But she wanted to be the happy spirit. And now she won't have anything to do with the play at all."

"Well, you can't worry about that," Carolyn advised. "I talked to her counselor. It seems Dinah doesn't work well with others. It's too bad you couldn't talk her into joining in, but if she refuses to cooperate there's nothing you can do.

Cooperation and teamwork are very important in putting on a play."

"I know." But Katie shook her head regretfully. "She would have been awfully good, though."

"Oh, I'm sure you'll do just fine without her," Carolyn said.

"But it can't be just fine," Katie responded. "It's got to be great." She looked out at the kids in the pool and frowned. "You know, they should be using this time to memorize their lines instead of playing in the pool."

"But you can't expect the girls to give up everything for the play," Carolyn noted. "And neither should you. Why don't you take a break and hop in the pool for a while?"

Katie was dying to take her up on that. But she shook her head. "No, I'm responsible for this play. And if it's going to be a success, I'm going to have to make some sacrifices." She felt terribly noble. "And I'm expecting the others to make some sacrifices too."

Carolyn smiled. "Well, don't expect too many. Nobody's going to want to give up every camp activity for the play."

"But it's going to take a lot of work," Katie argued.

"I realize that," Carolyn replied. "But remember, Katie, this Spectacular thing is supposed to be fun! Don't get yourself in a stew over it." She went back to the pool and dived in. And Katie returned to reading the script.

She didn't get very far. Maura and Andrea, two of the girls from cabin nine, sauntered by and paused in front of her. "Why, hello, Katie," Andrea said with a phony smile. "Why aren't you in the water splashing everyone as usual?"

Katie eyed them stonily. She really disliked those girls. "I'm working on our Spectacular project."

"Oh, my," Maura said in exaggerated awe. "Gee, I hope whatever you guys are doing is just as fabulous as what you did last year."

Remembering the fiasco of their singing efforts made Katie burn. "We're doing something very different this year." She couldn't resist adding, "and it's a lot more impressive than a fashion show."

Maura and Andrea exchanged looks, and their lips twitched as if they wanted to laugh. Without another word, they turned and continued their promenade around the pool.

Creeps, Katie thought. She'd show them. Her gang was going to have the most fantastic Spectacular act this camp had ever seen. She didn't care how many free swims she had to miss. Or horseback riding, or arts and crafts, or anything. She'd get the others to work really hard too. And she made a silent vow—this play would be the Spectacular event everyone would be talking about for years to come.

Trina got out of the water and joined Katie on the landing. "What did *they* want?"

"Oh, they were just being their usual obnoxious selves. Listen, have you started getting all the props we'll need together yet?"

"Well, no," Trina said. "But we'll start as soon as we figure out what we need. Karen and I have decided to do props and settings together. We're going to get Donna, in arts and crafts, to help us."

Katie beamed. She knew she could count on Trina to do her work well. And since she was Katie's best friend, Katie felt she could rely on Trina to support her and help her get the others to work hard too.

Of course, she knew they'd all want the play to be a hit. But would they work hard enough to make it one? Well, they absolutely had to. And she'd make sure they did.

When the group gathered in the dining hall that afternoon, Katie decided she'd start off with a pep talk to get everyone in the right frame of mind. But first she had to get their attention. Fran and Becky were bent over a comic book and giggling. Erin was brushing her hair. Megan had just come from a tennis game, and she was practicing her serves against a wall. The others were all over the room, talking.

"Can I have everyone's attention?" Katie called out. No one heard her. She tried again. "Everyone, come sit up here!" Still, there was no response.

Katie had been expecting this, and she was prepared. From under her tee shirt, she pulled out a whistle that hung from a chain around her neck. She'd saved it from the color war, and now she was glad she had. She put the whistle to her lips.

The shrill screech worked. Everyone stopped what she was doing. "Okay, everyone, take a seat up front."

Once they were settled in the semicircle of chairs, she began. "We've got a lot of work ahead of us, and I'm expecting all of you to work hard. And if we all work really, really hard, we can make this play the very best event at Spectacular. And that's what we all want, right?"

She would have liked a more enthusiastic response, maybe a cheer or two, but she had to be satisfied with the general nodding of heads.

"What do we win?" Becky asked.

Katie looked at her blankly. "What?"

"If we're the best and we win the Spectacular, what do we get?"

Katie realized this must be Becky's first year at Sunnyside. "Oh, it's not a contest. There's no winner."

"Then how come we have to be the best?"

"Because . . . because . . . we want to," Katie replied lamely. "And besides, Sarah worked very hard writing this play. And if we don't do a great job putting it on, no one will know how great the play is. Right, Sarah?"

Sarah smiled modestly. "Well, I don't know if it's a great play. I mean, I think it's a *good* play, but—"

"We can *make* it great," Katie said firmly. "But only if we work, work, work. Now, today we're going to go through the whole play on the stage. You can use your scripts and read from them. But by tomorrow, you should all have your lines memorized."

"By *tomorrow?*" Jenny looked aghast. "How can we memorize all these lines by tomorrow?"

"Yeah, and there's a movie at the lake tonight," Erin added. "There's not enough time."

"You can skip the movie," Katie began, but a chorus of protests drowned her out.

"Look, it's only one week till the Spectacular," Katie said. "You've got to learn your lines fast!" But from their expressions, she realized that was going to be impossible. "Okay," she

44

relented, "the day after tomorrow. All of you have to know your parts by Saturday."

Megan looked dismayed. "Are we going to have a rehearsal on Saturday? There's a trip to Pine Ridge on Saturday."

This time Katie stood firm. "You'll have to miss it. We have to rehearse every day if this play's going to be perfect in a week. C'mon, you guys, you have to cooperate!"

She ignored the whispered grumbling. "Let's get started. Fran, Becky, Jill, and Megan, go up to that side of the stage. Erin, you go to the other side."

They obeyed. Katie consulted her script. "Now, you four are supposed to be playing."

The four girls looked at her in confusion. "Playing what?" Becky asked.

"We could be holding hands and going around in a circle," Fran suggested. "Like ring-around-a-rosy."

Katie shook her head. "You'll get dizzy."

"Jumping rope?" Megan offered.

Katie considered that. "No, too noisy. The audience won't be able to hear what you're saying."

"What about 'London Bridge is Falling Down'?" Sarah asked.

Katie pictured that in her head. "Perfect!"

"That's so babyish," Erin complained.

45

"Well, they can't just be sitting there playing Monopoly or something," Katie stated. "We need action. They'll be playing, and Erin will wave her wand over them."

"What am I supposed to use for a wand?" Erin asked.

"We'll make you one," Trina called out.

"Just pretend for now," Katie told her. "Okay, let's try it."

Fran and Becky put their scripts down on the floor and formed an arc with their arms. Megan and Jill began to walk under the arc.

"Sing," Katie ordered them. In ragged voices, they began chanting the London Bridge song. Meanwhile, Erin waved her arm back and forth.

Suddenly, Megan stopped. "Erin, what are you doing?"

"Waving my wand, dummy."

Megan giggled. "You look like you're conducting an orchestra. Maybe you should just hold it up in the air or pointed at us."

"Hey!" Katie exclaimed. "You can't stop in the middle of a rehearsal like this!"

Megan's smile faded. "Okay, okay. You don't have to yell, you know. I can hear perfectly well."

"I'm sorry," Katie said. "But wait till we take a break to make suggestions, okay? We have to run through this whole script, and we can't have

46

interruptions." She consulted her script. "Fran, you're Gina. You've got the first line."

Awkwardly, Fran kept one arm up while she reached down with the other for her script. In trying to reach, with her other hand still clinging in the air with Becky's, she practically pulled Becky down to the floor.

Becky started giggling, and Katie clapped her hands sharply. "Be serious! Now, you see why you have to get your lines memorized fast? It's too hard to go through the play if you're always having to look at your scripts."

"My arm's getting tired," Erin complained, still waving it in a circle.

Katie grimaced. Erin was famous for complaining. And Katie began to fear she was going to hold up every rehearsal with her whining. "Just point it for a while," Katie said. "You wouldn't have to wave it for so long if you guys would cooperate and stop being silly. We should have already finished this scene by now. Come on, Fran, read your line."

Now Fran and Becky each had scripts in one hand, with the other two hands joined in the arc. Megan and Jill were still walking under the arc and around as Fran read the first line of the play. " 'Isn't this fun?' "

No one responded. Katie checked the script. "Megan, it's your line!"

"Oh. Sorry. Walking in circles like this is getting me dizzy." She looked at the script. " 'Yes, we always have fun together.' "

There was another silence. "Who's Tina?" Fran asked.

"Becky," Katie said. "C'mon, you guys should at least know the names of your parts by now!"

Becky shrugged apologetically. Then she read from her script. " 'It's nice that we always have good times together and never fight.' "

That sounded stiff and awkward to Katie. It was the kind of line that would make the audience groan. "Hold it," she said, and turned to Sarah. "Could we change that? Maybe have her say something like, 'It's really neat the way we never get into big fights or hassle each other.' "

"Hey, how come you can interrupt the play and we can't?" Becky asked.

"Because I'm the director," Katie said patiently. "That's my job. Sarah, is it okay if we change that?"

Sarah's face was troubled. "I like it the way it is."

Katie could understand that. After all, she wrote it, and she was proud of her work. Maybe she should just let it go as it was. She didn't want to insult Sarah.

But on the other hand, improving the play

48

was more important. "Please, Sarah," she wheedled. "It's better for the play."

Maybe she didn't say it right. Now Sarah actually looked upset. "Well, if you think you can write better than I do, go ahead." But her tone made it very clear she wasn't at all pleased with the change.

Katie swallowed. But then she remembered what she'd told herself. Personal feelings had to be put aside for the good of the play. She went up to the edge of the stage and handed a pencil to Becky. "Change the line to, 'It's really neat the way we never get into big fights or hassle each other.'"

The rehearsal went on, but it didn't get much smoother. Megan kept going off into a fog and didn't follow the script. When Jenny entered as the mean spirit, she was acting more like a lion or a tiger than a fantasy creature. Erin's complaints became more and more frequent.

By the final scene, when the group rescued the happy spirit, they were all exhausted. And Katie was getting really nervous. Of course, she didn't expect them to be perfect the first day. But now it seemed they would need even more practice than she thought.

" 'We cannot live without you,' " Becky read in a tired, dull-sounding voice. " 'We fight all the time, and nothing is fun anymore.' "

49

Silence followed her words. Katie consulted the script. "Megan! It's your line!"

She wasn't aware of how rough she sounded until she realized that Megan looked really upset. "Don't yell at me," she said in a quavering voice.

Katie gritted her teeth. "Just pay attention and follow the script, okay?"

Megan managed to get her next line out. Then Erin read her speech about loving each other and working things out for yourselves. And finally, it was over.

"We'll meet at the same time tomorrow," Katie told the group. "And remember to study your lines."

"It wouldn't kill you to say 'please,'" Jill muttered.

Katie rolled her eyes. "Okay, please learn your lines by Saturday. Are you happy now?"

Jill didn't look particularly happy. And Katie couldn't help noticing that none of the others did either.

"How did your first rehearsal go?" Carolyn asked them at dinner that evening.

"Not so great," Megan said.

Katie shot her a fierce look. She didn't want Carolyn to think she wasn't doing well. "It was just kind of rough," she said quickly. "Everything will go smoother once everyone learns her lines."

"The way Katie rewrites them," Sarah muttered.

"Sarah, I'm not going to rewrite all your lines!" Katie exclaimed. "I just thought that one little change would be an improvement."

"What do you think I should wear as the Spirit of Happiness?" Erin asked.

Costumes! Katie hadn't thought about that at all yet. "Trina, you and Karen should ask Donna if she can help us with that. Maybe she's got some stuff in her storage room. You can do that tomorrow."

"Yes, ma'am," Trina replied. Katie eyed her curiously. What was that "ma'am" business supposed to mean? Okay, maybe she was coming on a little too strong. But there was only a week to prepare and a lot to do.

Everyone at dinner seemed more quiet than usual. Katie figured they were all probably just tired. She was pretty tired herself. But Megan, in particular, was acting odd. She barely spoke to Katie at all. And every time their eyes met, Megan looked away.

After dinner, as they were headed back to the cabin, Katie pulled her aside. "What's wrong with you?"

She was alarmed to see what looked like a

hint of tears in Megan's eyes. "Are you going to keep yelling at me like you did today?"

Megan could be so babyish sometimes. "Megan, I have to tell you when you're doing something wrong."

"Then just tell me. You don't have to scream."

"Oh, Megan, don't take it so personally! We have to move this along quickly, and sometimes I just can't waste time being polite. But okay. I'll try not to yell so much."

"Good. Because this isn't going to be much fun if you're going to be yelling all the time."

They walked along together silently. Katie had an uncomfortable feeling, like she'd just lied to Megan. Of course, she hadn't promised she wouldn't yell. She'd only said she'd try not to. But Megan had better get used to some yelling. Because if this play was going to be any good, Katie had a feeling she'd be doing a lot of it.

# Chapter 5

On Saturday morning, Katie was the first to wake up. But she didn't jump out of bed. She just lay there with her eyes closed, unwilling to let go of her dream.

It was the night of the Sunnyside Spectacular. There'd been singers, dancers, a fashion show, and all of them had been greeted with polite applause. And then came "The Battle of the Spirits."

In her mind, she saw the curtain rise on the magical scene, the audience captivated by the Spirit of Happiness waving her wand over the cheerful children playing. She could hear the gasp of horror as the Spirit of Meanness entered. She felt the tension building as the children argued and bickered. And she heard the sigh of relief as they finally rescued the spirit, and returned to being their happy selves.

Everything went perfectly. No one missed an entrance or a line. Excitement washed over the audience. And when it was over, there was a standing ovation.

Katie remembered going to a play once with her parents. The audience yelled bravo when the actors took their bows. That's what they'd do at the Spectacular. And then, just like at the play she saw, they'd yell, "Director! Director!"

She opened her eyes. No, that wasn't what they'd yelled. They'd called out, "Author! Author!" Well, Sarah deserved to get a bow. But she'd make sure there was someone in the audience who would call for "director" too!

But none of this was going to happen unless the play worked perfectly. So far, they'd had two full rehearsals. Less than a week remained before the performance. And the play was far from perfect.

Suddenly she sat up. "Guys, wake up! I've got an idea!"

A few bodies stirred, but no one got up. Katie climbed down her ladder and stood in the center of the cabin. "C'mon, everyone! Wake up!"

Now, her cabin mates began to react. Megan actually sat up and rubbed her eyes. Trina

hoisted herself up on her elbows. "What's the matter?" she mumbled sleepily.

"Let's ask Carolyn if we can get excused from all activities today. Then we could spend the whole day rehearsing, instead of just during free period."

Now everyone was sitting up. Erin looked aghast. "You want to rehearse all day?" She turned and peered out the window. "Are you nuts? The sun's out! It's going to be absolutely gorgeous today!"

Megan slipped out of bed and padded over to the bulletin board where the weekly schedule was posted. "We've got canoes this morning! I don't want to miss that."

"We're already missing the trip to Pine Ridge," Sarah pointed out. "We can't give up everything."

"And Stewart from Camp Eagle is coming over to play tennis with me this afternoon," Megan said. "If he shows up and I'm not there, he'll be furious. And I'll lose the best tennis player I've ever played with!"

Frustrated, Katie turned to Trina for support. But Trina just shrugged helplessly. "I don't think an all-day rehearsal is a good idea, Katie."

"But we need it," Katie insisted. "I'm willing

to give everything up. You guys should be too. I told you we'd have to make some sacrifices."

"Forget it," Erin said flatly. "Honestly, Katie, you're acting like this is a Broadway show or something. It's just the Spectacular."

Katie faced her sternly. "Well, if that's your attitude, maybe you shouldn't even be in the play!" She hadn't realized how loud they were getting until Carolyn's door opened and their sleepy-eyed counselor peered out.

"What's going on out here?"

"Katie wants us to spend the whole day practicing the play," Erin said.

Carolyn raised her eyebrows. "The whole day? That's seems like a lot of rehearsal. Katie, you don't need that much time, do you? How long is the play anyway?"

"Twenty minutes," Sarah said. "We're already practicing every day during free period."

"And Katie's been making us recite our lines during rest time too," Megan put in.

Katie glared at her. Carolyn wasn't supposed to know that.

Carolyn looked at Katie reprovingly. "Now, Katie, you know you're all supposed to be quiet during rest time. And I'm not giving you permission to get out of all the other camp activities."

"We don't need that much rehearsal anyway," Erin said. "We're doing enough already."

"Oh yeah?" Katie countered. "Well, I think you need it. You guys were no better onstage yesterday than you were the day before!"

A silence fell over the room. Carolyn cocked her head to the side and eyed Katie seriously. "Katie, could I talk with you for a minute? In my room?"

Katie could feel her face burning as she followed Carolyn into her room. Carolyn shut the door and motioned for Katie to sit on the bed beside her.

"Katie, remember when I told you how important it is to be tactful in this kind of situation? I realize you're concerned about the performance, but if you come on too strong, others are going to resent you."

Katie pressed her lips together tightly. Was this going to be a lecture? She didn't need to hear it. Besides, she knew all these girls a lot better than Carolyn did. She knew that sometimes they needed to be pushed.

"You know," Carolyn continued, "my mother had a saying. 'You can catch more flies with honey than with vinegar.' Do you know what that means?"

Katie had heard that expression before too. She nodded in resignation. "I should be all sweet

57

and gushy and beg them to follow my directions instead of ordering them."

"Well, not exactly. But you could be more gentle and understanding."

Katie sat silently for a minute. "Okay," she said finally and without much enthusiasm. "I'll try. But this play's never going to come off if I don't get some cooperation from the other girls."

Carolyn smiled slightly. "Just remember, Katie. Kids come to summer camp to have fun."

Katie looked at her blankly. What did fun have to do with this? They had work to do.

She went back out into the main room, where everyone was getting ready for breakfast. "We'll just be rehearsing during free period," she announced. The look of relief on their faces was annoying. She raised her voice, and added, "Everyone better be on time! And know your lines!" She hoped she sounded authoritative and maybe even a little threatening.

No one offered any arguments. But nobody looked threatened either. Or even impressed.

Later that morning, out in a canoe with Trina, she expressed her fears. "I'm really getting worried about this play. No one's acting like it's important. And if we do a crummy performance, I'll look really stupid. I mean, we all will. Just like last year." She gazed around the lake, at the girls in the other canoes. "Right this minute, they should all be practicing their lines."

"Good grief," Trina said mildly, "you're acting like this is the most important event of the summer. It's just supposed to be fun. It's not that big of a deal."

"It is a big deal to me," Katie insisted. "And it should be to you too! Am I the only one taking this seriously? Do you want to get laughed at again, like last year?"

"Oh, come on, Katie, the audience laughed at just about everyone. Except that ballet dancer. You were just upset because it was your idea and it didn't work very well. You shouldn't be so uptight this time. After all, the play isn't your idea."

"But I'm the director. And if we're a flop, everyone's going to blame me. Remember when I was a captain in the color war? If my team had lost, they all would have said it was my fault. And I had to really push those other kids to win, remember?"

"I remember," Trina said softly. And then Katie remembered something. Trina hadn't been on her team. She'd been on the other side. And Katie had tried to get Trina to lose some events on purpose so Katie's team could win.

The memory filled her with shame. And suddenly she began pulling at her paddle fiercely.

"Look, Katie," Trina said, "there's a big difference between this show and color war. Color war was a competition. This isn't. It's easier to get people to work hard when there's a question of winning or losing. Like I said, this is just supposed to be fun. No one expects that much from a Spectacular act. There's no winner."

"I know, I know." But Katie knew something else too. There were always one or two Spectacular events everyone talked about for summers after. Like the ballet dancer last year. She wanted all of Sunnyside to be talking about their play. And saying it was the best Spectacular event ever.

"It's almost time for lunch," Katie noted. They steered the canoe around and started heading for shore.

"Look," Trina said. "There's that girl from cabin five. What was her name?"

Katie peered toward the bank. "Dinah." She was sitting alone, curled up and staring out at the water with her arms wrapped around her knees. "Boy, I wish she was in the play. She would have been better than Jenny."

"Karen told me Dinah just doesn't get along with other people," Trina said. "She wouldn't even participate in the color war. I think she's one of those people who doesn't care about hav-

60

ing any friends. She likes being alone all the time."

Katie shook her head in amazement. "I feel sorry for her. Not having any friends, not being part of anything—I can't imagine what that would feel like."

Trina nodded. "Pretty awful, I guess."

Worse than awful, Katie thought. Totally unimaginable.

Katie checked the clock again on the dining hall wall. Only about half the kids were there. And she'd specifically told them to be on time! "Where is everyone?" she asked Sarah.

"Trina and Karen are over at arts and crafts, working on scenery. I'm sure the others are on their way."

Katie wondered how she could sound so calm. After all, it was her play. Wasn't she getting worried about it at all?

As each latecomer straggled in, she fixed a stern look on her. None of them seemed terribly concerned though.

"Where's Erin?" Katie demanded. "She's ten minutes late! And we can't start without her!"

"Hey, you guys, wait till you see what I got!" Erin came running into the rehearsal with something draped across her arm. "Donna found this for me in the arts and crafts storage room.

61

She's got lots of old costumes from plays in there. And this fits me!" She held it up.

Katie joined the others gathered around her. "You're late," she accused Erin.

Erin shrugged. "Just a few minutes. And look at this!" The dress was made of some thin, soft material, pale blue, with glitter all over it.

"I'm going to wear it in the play," Erin said. "Isn't it perfect?"

Sarah nodded approvingly. "It's exactly right."

"It's nice," Katie admitted. "But Erin, I told you guys you have to be on time from now on."

"Okay, okay," Erin murmured, but she was still admiring the dress. Katie groaned silently. It was so typical of Erin to be more concerned with how she looked than how the play was performed.

She turned to the group. "Okay, everyone get up on the stage. And leave your scripts down here."

Megan's hand flew to her mouth. She looked frightened. "What if we forget a line?"

"You were supposed to have learned them all by today," Katie reminded her. But Sarah stepped in.

"I'll call out your line if you forget it."

Katie glanced at her in annoyance. If Sarah was going to feed them their lines, they'd never learn them! But Sarah just went with them up to the stage and sat on the side with a script in her lap.

The girls gathered on the stage and began the first scene. To Katie's surprise, it went pretty well. Megan only messed up one line. Then Jenny, as the Spirit of Meanness, entered.

"Wait a minute," Katie called out. "Jenny, you can't just walk on normally like that. You have to look mean."

"How do I do that?" Jenny asked.

Katie thought about it. "Try hunching your shoulders and putting out your arms. And take long, slithery steps, like this." And she demonstrated the walk.

"Ooh, that looks good," Sarah called from the stage.

Jenny tried to imitate Katie's walk. She got the arm position right, but she didn't hunch her shoulders. And her slither looked more like she was pretending to be skating.

"No, no," Katie said. "Like this. Hunch your shoulders."

She made Jenny do it over and over again, until she got it right. But she still looked worried. "I don't know if I can remember to do all that at the same time."

"Sure you can," Katie said. "But you have to

63

keep practicing. After this rehearsal, I'll work with you some more on it."

"I can't stay after rehearsal!" Jenny exclaimed. "I've got archery."

"I'm sure you can get out of it if you ask your counselor," Katie replied.

"But I don't want to get out of it. I love archery!"

Katie gritted her teeth. "Look, I'm just trying to get you to do this right! If you can't stay, then practice on your own. But you'd better do it right tomorrow. Now, let's go on with the play."

They continued. Jenny announced her presence, and Erin tried to send her away. They pretended to struggle. Erin was supposed to yell, "Stop! Stop!" Instead, she started giggling.

"Erin! What are you doing?" Katie asked. "You're not supposed to be giggling."

"I can't help it. She's tickling me!"

"Jenny, don't tickle her," Katie ordered.

"I wasn't doing it on purpose!"

"Then just grab her by the hand and pull her offstage," Katie said.

Jenny grabbed Erin's hand and yanked. Erin immediately lost her balance and fell down. And everyone cracked up.

"C'mon, you guys, get serious!" Katie yelled.

"What if that happened in the middle of the performance?"

"It would be pretty funny." Megan giggled.

Katie glared at her. "No, it wouldn't."

Somehow, Jenny managed to get Erin offstage, and the play went on. Now that the Spirit of Happiness was gone, the group onstage stopped getting along.

" 'Let's play tag,' " Jill said.

" 'You're it,' " Fran returned.

" 'I don't want to be it,' " Jill said. " 'Tina, you're it.' "

" 'Not me,' " Becky said. " 'Make Sandy be it.' "

Megan stood there, looking blank.

"Megan, it's your line!" Katie yelled. From the side of the stage, Sarah hissed, " 'I don't feel like playing at all.' "

" 'I don't feel like playing at all,' " Megan said. " 'I feel too sad.' "

Jill ran over to Fran and touched her shoulder. " 'You're it. C'mon, everyone.' "

" 'But I think Tina should be it,' " Fran complained. She touched Becky's shoulder. Becky acted like she'd been hit hard and fell down. " 'Hey, you hit me!' " Then she got up and tapped Megan. " 'Sandy, you're it.' "

Megan hesitated. Katie was about to remind her that she had the next line, but Megan remembered. " 'I'm not going to be it. I want to play hopscotch.' "

" 'That's a stupid game,' " Becky said.

There was a second of silence. "Megan!" Katie yelled. Megan flinched, but she spoke her line. " 'Hopscotch is not stupid! *You're* stupid!' "

" 'No, I'm not!' " Becky exclaimed. " 'You're stupid!' "

Again, there was a silence. "Megan!" Katie yelled.

Sarah hissed something at her. " 'I am *not* stupid!' " Megan called back to Becky.

" 'You're the most stupid person in the world,' " Fran said to Becky.

" 'Oh, yeah? Well, you're stupid and dumb and ugly, too!' " Becky said back.

" 'I'm not as dumb and ugly as she is,' " Fran retorted, pointing to Megan.

Megan stood still. Sarah was saying something from the side of the stage, but she couldn't hear her.

"Megan!" Katie yelled. "I told you to learn your lines! What's the matter with you anyway?"

And Megan burst into tears. Then she turned, ran down the stage stairs, and out the dining hall.

Katie watched in amazement. Then she

66

turned to the others on the stage. "What's the matter with her?"

"You yelled at her," Sarah said. "You know Megan doesn't like to be yelled at."

Katie did know that. And she felt bad inside. But she was beginning to lose patience. "Well, if she doesn't want to be yelled at, she should learn her lines!" She checked her script. "Becky, you have the next line."

Becky's voice had lost its expression. " 'If you don't want to do what I want to do, I don't want to play with any of you anymore.' "

Katie considered this line. It sounded confusing to her. "Sarah, let's change this to something like, 'You're all creeps. I'm not hanging out with you anymore.' "

Becky frowned and looked at her doubtfully. "But I already learned my lines. If you change them now, I'll get confused."

"She's right," Sarah said. "I think it's too late to change lines now."

"But it's better for the play," Katie insisted.

"I don't think it makes that big a difference," Sarah said.

Katie couldn't believe this. Here she was, trying to improve the play, and nobody seemed to care! She threw up her hands.

"Look, we can't do much more without Megan here. Let's meet again after dinner."

A chorus of groans greeted that suggestion. This annoyed Katie even more. "Just be here at six-thirty," she ordered them. And she walked out of the room.

When she left the dining hall, she went directly to the arts and crafts building. Inside, some of the younger campers were gathered at a table with Donna, who was showing them how to make pot holders on looms. When Donna saw Katie, she pointed a finger toward one of the back rooms.

Katie expected to see Trina and Karen hard at work painting the backdrop for the play. But when she reached the doorway and peered in, her mouth dropped open. There, against one wall, was the long length of cardboard, with trees lightly sketched on it. Only one had been painted, though.

And there were Trina and Karen—but they weren't painting. Trina was standing on her head. "See, you have to keep your hands the right length apart to keep your balance."

"Let me try it." And Karen bent over, placed her hands on the floor, and lifted her legs above her head. They didn't get there, though. She toppled over, and sat on the floor, laughing. Then she saw Katie. "Oh, hi, Katie."

Trina dropped her legs and returned to an upright position. "Hi! Is the rehearsal over?"

Her mouth set in a grim line, Katie muttered, "Yes." Then she strode over to the practically blank backdrop. "Is this all you guys have done? You should be practically finished by now!"

"Sorry," Trina said. "We started talking about gymnastics, and—"

"I don't want any excuses! Do you realize we've only got a few days before the Spectacular?"

Trina seemed taken aback by her tone. "It's not going to take us long to finish, Katie."

"We just have to fill in the outline," Karen added.

"I want to see it done! Isn't anyone else working on this besides me?"

"Katie, calm down!" Trina exclaimed. "Everything's going to be okay."

"No, it won't! Not unless I get some cooperation! I want these sets done by tomorrow."

Trina put her hands on her hips. "Katie, what's the matter with you? You're acting like—like a dictator!"

Katie didn't know what to say. She felt like all control was slipping out of her hands. "Just—just do it, okay?"

She turned and walked out. Her head was a jumble of feelings. Trina—her best friend—had just called her a dictator! What was the matter with everyone? Why couldn't they just do what they were supposed to do?

She made her way back toward the cabin. She was feeling so confused she didn't see Carolyn until she almost bumped directly into her.

"Katie! Is something wrong?"

Katie gazed into her counselor's warm eyes. "Everything's wrong!" she cried out. "They won't listen to me! They're all being totally uncooperative! And I don't know what to do." It was all she could do to keep from bursting out in tears.

Carolyn's face was compassionate. "Oh, Katie, I'm sorry. What happened?"

Katie didn't feel like going into details. "They just won't listen to me. I had to cancel the rehearsal!" She took a deep breath and tried to speak calmly. "We're meeting again after dinner tonight."

"Would you mind if I sat in?" Carolyn asked. "Maybe I can help out."

Katie felt totally confused. She didn't really want Carolyn watching their rehearsal. Counselors weren't supposed to be involved in the Spectacular. But if she did come, and she backed Katie up on her decisions, it could work to her advantage.

"Well, okay."

Carolyn smiled, and it made Katie feel a little better. They parted, and Katie continued on toward the cabin. Carolyn was okay. Maybe having her there would get the girls to listen to her.

Funny . . . she'd had no problem organizing the girls in the color war. Why was this so much harder?

# Chapter 6

The mood at that evening's rehearsal was subdued. And there was something in the air, some feeling Katie couldn't quite identify. All she knew was that it made her feel uncomfortable.

Onstage, the actors were gathered in a group, talking too softly for Katie to hear. They weren't laughing, they weren't even smiling. Were they talking about her? she wondered. Were they still griping about the afternoon rehearsal? No, they were probably just complaining about having an extra rehearsal. Well, that was just too bad, Katie thought. The way they'd been acting, Katie had a pretty strong suspicion they'd need lots of extra rehearsals before they'd be ready for the Spectacular.

Her eyes darted between the group onstage and Carolyn, sitting at a dining hall table. She had this sinking feeling that as soon as the rehearsal started, the girls were going to continue their usual whining and arguing and horsing around.

Sarah approached her. "How come Carolyn's here? We've never let counselors get involved with Spectacular acts before."

"I know," Katie said. "But I thought maybe having her here would keep everyone from behaving so badly."

Sarah looked doubtful. "I don't think they've been so awful. They just want to have a good time."

"Look, Sarah, this is your play. You want it to be a success onstage, right?"

"Sure."

"Then they've got to stop having their good times and start working! And if they won't listen to me, at least I've got Carolyn here to tell them they *have* to."

Sarah bit her lip. "Just don't make Megan cry again, okay?"

Katie sighed. "Look, Megan's just too sensitive. Now I'm trying to whip this play into shape, and I can't worry about people's feelings!"

She turned away from Sarah and briskly clapped her hands. "Okay, everyone," she called out, a little louder than usual. "We're going to run through the scene where the mean spirit comes out for the first time."

The girls got into their positions. Fran and Becky put their hands up together in the London Bridge position, while Megan and Jill walked under and around. Erin stood off to the side and held up the wand Karen had made. Jenny waited offstage for a second, and then walked on.

"Stop!" Katie yelled. "Jenny, why aren't you doing the walk we practiced this afternoon?"

Jenny's expression was abashed. "I guess I forgot how to do it."

"I told you to practice!"

"Hey!" Jill called down from the stage. "Stop yelling at my sister!"

"Well, if she did what she's supposed to do, I wouldn't have to yell!" She glanced over at Carolyn, hoping for a nod of approval. But Carolyn was just watching intently, and her brow was furrowed. She wants me to work this out for myself, Katie thought. And so she would.

"You do it like this," she said, trying to keep her voice at a reasonable level. She demonstrated the hunched, slithery walk. "Now, do your entrance again." For emphasis, she added, "And this time, do it right!"

Jenny did a feeble imitation of Katie's walk.

74

"Better," Katie said, "but not good enough. Okay, go on."

Erin turned and saw Jenny. She let out a loud gasp, dramatically clasped a hand to her heart, and took a step backward. " 'Who are you?' " she asked in a voice that reeked of horror and dismay.

"Stop!" Katie yelled. "Why are you guys giggling like that?"

"We couldn't help it," Jill said. "She looked funny."

Katie frowned. If Erin looked funny to them, she might look funny to the audience. And this wasn't supposed to be funny.

"Well, you can't giggle in the middle of the play like that. And Erin, you're showing off. Don't be so dramatic. The way you did that looked silly."

Erin's eyes shot daggers at her. "Carolyn, do you think that looked silly?"

Katie turned to look at Carolyn. Tell her I'm right, she silently pleaded.

"Not silly exactly," Carolyn said slowly. "But I think what Katie means is that it looks a little exaggerated to us. You want her to tone it down a little, don't you, Katie?"

"Yes," Katie replied. "That's just what I want her to do."

"Okay," Erin said. She went through it again,

75

without looking quite so dramatic, and it was much better. I was right, Katie thought with satisfaction. But why couldn't Erin just listen to me the first time?

" 'I am the Spirit of Meanness,' " Jenny growled. And then she let out a loud cackle.

"Wait a minute," Katie interrupted. "Why did you laugh like that?"

Jenny shrugged. "I don't know. It felt like the right thing to do."

Katie consulted the script. "It doesn't say anything about laughing here. Sarah, did you want her to laugh right here?"

"It's okay with me," Sarah called out. "Actually, I think it sounded kind of neat. Carolyn, how do you think Jenny's laugh sounded?"

"It's an artistic interpretation," Carolyn said. "An actor has to figure out the personality and motives of the character, and determine the best way to communicate the character to the audience."

That sounded like a lot of mumbo jumbo to Katie. But she understood what Carolyn meant, and she wasn't happy about it. If the actors could play the characters any way they wanted—it would be chaos! They could end up treating the whole play like a joke!

"Look, I don't know about this artistic interpretation stuff," she said. "I think you guys should just do what I tell you to."

Erin put her hands on her hips. "You mean, we don't get any say in how we play our parts?"

"I'm just doing what a director's supposed to do," Katie said. "Now, go on with the play."

They continued through the scene. Jenny dragged Erin to the back of the stage, pretended to tie her up, and then announced that she was taking over. Meanwhile, the others continued to play and acted like they were totally unaware of what was going on.

Jenny returned to center stage. " 'There will be no more happiness in this land. For I, the Spirit of Meanness, am in control now. And my power is great!' " She thrust out her arm toward the playing girls.

The girls began their argument about playing tag. At first, it went along okay, and then there was an awkward silence. Megan forgot a line again.

"Megan! It's your line!"

From the side of the stage, Sarah started to hiss Megan's line to her. But Katie stopped her. "She's got to learn these lines by heart. And she'll never do that if you keep helping her!"

She tried to ignore the fact that Megan's lower lip was trembling. "Look, Katie," Sarah said, "everyone's bound to forget a line or two."

"No they won't, not if they try harder," Katie retorted. "They're just not concentrating!"

She couldn't help but be aware of the cold looks everyone onstage was giving her. But she didn't let them bother her. "Okay, go on."

The girls continued, but not for long. "Stop!" Katie called out. "I've got an idea. Just arguing like that isn't enough. I think a real fight would be better. You should all start pushing and shoving each other."

She ran up to the stage. "Fran, when you say, 'You're it,' pretend to shove Jill. Then Jill will shove you back. Megan and Becky, keep pushing each other back and forth. When Jill shoves Fran, Fran can bump into Megan. Then Megan, you get angry, and pretend to push Fran away."

"Wait a minute," Megan said. "This is getting too confusing."

"Yeah," Jill said. "I won't be able to remember my lines if I have to think about pushing people too."

"But this would make the scene better!" Katie insisted. "The audience will be able to see how the mean spirit is affecting everyone. Sarah, don't you like that idea?"

"I don't think they have to push and shove," Sarah said. "I think arguing and yelling at each other is enough for the audience to get the message."

Katie was getting seriously frustrated. "But the play needs more action. It's boring if all they do is talk. Carolyn, don't you think I'm right?"

"It's not a bad idea," Carolyn said, "but Megan and Jill have a point. It would be hard for them all to remember what to do and what to say at the same time."

"It wouldn't be so hard if they practiced harder," Katie argued vehemently. "They don't want to work hard enough to make this play a success! They're just being lazy, that's all!"

"We are not!" Jenny yelled.

"Then do what I say and stop arguing!" Katie yelled back.

"Since when do you give all the orders?" Erin asked loudly.

Katie threw up her hands in exasperation and turned to Carolyn. "Aren't they supposed to listen to me? Isn't the director supposed to give the orders?"

Carolyn's reply was quiet and thoughtful. "Well, the director should make suggestions, certainly. But she ought to listen to all points of view, too."

This is ridiculous, Katie thought furiously. If she listened to all points of view, they'd never get anywhere! They'd end up taking a vote on everything!

She turned back to the girls on the stage. "Look, I'm supposed to be the director, and the director is supposed to be in charge. I'm sick and tired of all this fussing!"

She knew she was shouting, but she didn't care. She had to shake them up.

But none of them looked shook up. Not even Megan.

It was time for an ultimatum. Katie put her hands on her hips, held her head up high, and spoke with as much authority as she could muster. "Okay, here's the deal. If you guys don't start cooperating, you're all going to make fools of yourselves at the Spectacular. Either you all agree to start listening to me and stop being silly or I quit. You can just do the play any way you want to do it and I'll get out of here."

She waited for expressions of dismay, cries of protest, pleas for her to stay on. They had to realize how much they needed her.

But no one said a word. All the girls on the stage just looked back at her, silently. Katie could feel disbelief and fury rise up inside of her.

"Okay, if that's the way you want it, you can all direct yourselves!" She whirled around and headed for the door. Even as she crossed the dining hall, she expected to hear them calling her back. But the room remained silent.

They'll be sorry, Katie thought angrily as she crossed the campgrounds toward her cabin. Now they've got no one to lead them, no one to organize them. They'll probably have to drop out of the Spectacular. And if they don't, the play will be a disaster. The audience will jeer them, and they'll be the laughingstock of the whole Spectacular. And as long as no one at camp thought Katie had anything to do with it, she didn't care.

Cabin six was empty. Katie climbed the ladder to her bed, and lay there facedown. She felt as if a huge gray cloud had suddenly fallen on her head. How could they do this to her? She, Katie Dillon, who had always been the cabin six leader, the one who gave out advice, the one all the others listened to—she was being rejected! There was a great big lump in her throat. It wasn't something she felt very often, but when she did, she knew what would come next. And all of a sudden, she started to cry.

But just then, the door opened, and Trina walked in. Katie sat up quickly, hoping there was no suspicious redness in her eyes.

Trina was surprised to see her. "What are

you doing here? Isn't there a rehearsal going on?"

Katie nodded. "I quit."

"You quit!"

"Yeah. They wouldn't listen to me, and I was sick of fighting with them. So I walked out."

She waited for Trina to say something like, "How stupid of them," or, "The play will be a big flop now." But Trina just looked at her sadly. "Oh, Katie," she murmured, and shook her head.

Katie was startled. The least she expected was for Trina to try and talk her into going back. It was really strange. Trina didn't even seem dismayed.

She's probably still angry because I yelled at her about the scenery, Katie thought. Well, I won't be yelling at her anymore. And they probably aren't going to need any scenery anyway.

"Actually, I don't even care," she said nonchalantly. "It's a dumb play. Hey, you want to go over to the activities hall and play Ping-Pong?"

"I can't. I just came back to get some marking pens I left here. Karen and I are making crowns."

"Crowns? For what?"

"A gold glitter one for the happy spirit, and a black one for the mean spirit."

Katie was about to suggest that they make a scary mask for the mean spirit instead, and then she remembered. It was none of her business anymore. "You know, that might be a waste of time. I don't even see how they can put on a play without a director."

Trina didn't respond. She collected her pens, but she paused by their bunk before she left. "If you'd like, you can come back with me. We could always use more help with the scenery."

Katie shook her head. "I don't want to have anything to do with it. It's going to be a terrible play."

Trina shrugged. "Okay. See you later."

After she left, Katie just lay there for another minute. Then she pulled herself up and climbed down the ladder. She wasn't going to let the others come back and find her lying there, looking depressed.

She headed over to the activities hall. Maybe she'd find someone else who wasn't involved in the Spectacular, someone she could hang around with.

There were a lot of kids in the game room, but they weren't just hanging around. They were practicing some sort of fancy square dance. One girl stood apart from them, calling out steps. "And smile," she yelled. "There's going to be a big audience watching you!" Katie's eyes roamed the dancers. They were all smiling. It seemed this group didn't have any problem taking directions.

She wandered over to one of the smaller rooms and stood in the entrance. The cabin seven girls were there. There was a Michael Jackson tape on a cassette player, and one girl was trying to do his famous moonwalking step.

"That's great!" another girl squealed. But then the Michael Jackson girl tripped over her own feet, and everyone started laughing. "Not bad for the first time," another camper said encouragingly. "C'mon, try it again."

They looked like they were having fun. Katie watched for a few more minutes. The girl who seemed to be in charge worked with the dancing girl for a while. The dancing girl didn't complain or argue with her or anything like that.

It was just Katie's bad luck that she'd gotten stuck with a bunch of girls who couldn't get along. And now, for the first time since she'd come to Sunnyside, she wouldn't even be part of the Spectacular. And she hated not being a part of something that used to be so much fun.

It wasn't fair. All she wanted was for her

group to do a great show. She would have done anything to help them. All these other groups—they looked like they really cared about their performances. Why couldn't her group care too?

Katie felt that lump in her throat again. And she hurried away, before anyone could see what she knew was sure to follow.

# Chapter 7

It was as if Katie were suddenly surrounded by strangers. These girls, her cabin mates, her best summer friends—they were like people she barely knew. That night, the next morning, through breakfast, swimming, and archery, she felt like an outsider, someone who didn't belong.

They weren't exactly snubbing her. They said good night, and good morning, and pass the salt—that sort of thing. But for the most part, they were all pretty quiet. Katie knew why. They probably wanted to talk about the play, to ask her to come back and help them, but they were too proud. And she certainly wasn't going to bring up the subject.

But as they were standing in the line at lunch, she couldn't resist mentioning it to Megan, who was standing behind her. She tried to sound very casual, as if she didn't care at all. "Are you guys rehearsing this afternoon?"

Megan nodded, her eyes firmly fixed on the floor. Poor Megan, Katie thought. She was probably scared the play would be a flop too.

Then Megan mumbled something Katie couldn't hear. "What did you say?"

"Carolyn's going to direct us."

Katie's mouth dropped open. They were going to let Carolyn direct them? She couldn't believe it. Except for the youngest kids, it was considered really dorky to let a counselor be involved in your Spectacular act.

Surprise wasn't the only reaction she had. She felt anger, too. Carolyn should have supported her and convinced the others to listen to her. And instead she was just taking over!

When she emerged from the line with her tray, she paused. While the others headed directly for their usual table, she just stood there. She didn't want to sit with her cabin mates. She felt like they were all a bunch of traitors.

Her eyes scanned the dining hall for someone to sit with. And then she spotted Dinah, the girl from cabin five, sitting all alone. She made her way over to her table.

"Hi, can I sit here?"

Dinah looked at her with an expression that wasn't very friendly. "If you're going to try to talk me into playing the Spirit of Meanness, forget it."

"I'm not even involved in the play anymore," Katie said. Without waiting for Dinah's permission she sat down.

There was a glimmer of interest in Dinah's eyes. "How come?"

"Because they wouldn't cooperate and listen to me. So I'm dropping out of the whole Spectacular thing."

Dinah took a delicate sip of her milk and set the carton down. "The whole Spectacular thing sounds pretty stupid, anyway."

Katie shrugged. "Sometimes it's fun. Not this year, though." She wondered what Dinah did during free period when everyone else was at rehearsal. It was something she ought to find out. She wasn't going to have anything to do during free period either.

"What do you do when everyone's rehearsing?"

"I go over to the activities hall and see if anyone wants to play checkers."

Checkers. Katie had always considered that an incredibly boring game. "Do you want to meet me there today and play Ping-Pong?"

"No, I don't like Ping-Pong. But I'll play checkers with you."

Katie grimaced. "I don't much like checkers.

How about this—I'll play a game of checkers with you, and then we can play Ping-Pong."

Dinah shook her head. "Are you deaf? I *said*, I didn't like Ping-Pong. I only want to play checkers."

Katie looked at Dinah in amazement. Hadn't this girl ever heard of compromises? Another thought occurred to her. "Why are you sitting all alone?"

"Because I don't have any friends here." She said this as if she were proud of the fact. "I'm a loner. I'm not into group activities."

"Then why did you come to camp?"

"My parents made me. They think I should learn to get along with other people. But what's the point? If you start hanging around with other people, you end up doing what they want to do instead of what you want to do."

That sounded a little weird to Katie. "Well, it's not always that way. I mean, sometimes you get your friends to do what you want, and sometimes you do what they want. You take turns."

Dinah sniffed. "I only do what *I* want."

The girl was really obnoxious, Katie decided. No wonder she didn't have any friends.

They ate the rest of the meal in silence. When lunch was over, Katie asked, "What do you have now?"

"Arts and crafts."

"Me too." Katie glanced back to her regular table. Her cabin mates were getting up. She'd been dreading arts and crafts. She suspected that all the cabin six girls would be helping Trina paint scenery.

"I'll walk over there with you," Katie told Dinah. Dinah didn't offer any objection, though she didn't look particularly pleased at the prospect either. They walked together, but they might as well have been walking alone. It was impossible to make conversation with this unfriendly girl.

When they entered the arts and crafts cabin, Katie saw that her suspicions were correct. Inside, she watched all the cabin six girls head toward the back room. That was where Trina and Karen had been making the scenery.

She wondered how it all looked. She was dying to go back and peek in, but she didn't want the others to think she was interested.

The cabin five girls were in the cabin too, but they were gathered at the other end of the room around a big table. Katie wondered why they weren't helping with the scenery too.

"What are they doing?" she asked Dinah.

"It's a special project," Dinah replied. "They're learning how to make a quilt."

"Oh, yeah?" Katie asked with interest. That

sounded kind of neat. "How come you're not working on it?"

Dinah explained. "When we first started, we had to choose a pattern. I picked a particular pattern, but no one else liked it. So I told them, if they didn't make the quilt I wanted to make, I wouldn't work on it at all."

Katie was dumbfounded. This girl was even stranger than she thought. Why would anyone make such a fuss over a silly thing like a quilt pattern?

Dinah went over to the jewelry table, where no one else was sitting. She sat down, and started stringing beads. Turning away, Katie saw Laura, the cabin five counselor.

"What's the matter with that Dinah anyway?" she asked Laura. "Doesn't she like doing anything with other people?"

Laura sighed. "Not really. She's a loner, and she actually seems content being the way she is. Maybe someday she'll realize how important it is to get along with other people. But I don't think that will happen this summer."

Katie couldn't understand this. She turned back and looked at Dinah, sitting there all alone, stringing her beads. A wave of sadness passed over her. Dinah might be sullen and unfriendly, but Katie felt sorry for her. She couldn't imagine how anyone could be that stuck in her ways, content without friends, without being a part of whatever was going on . . .

She couldn't look at Dinah any longer. It made her feel too creepy. Was that how *she* was going to end up? Alone and friendless?

No, never, she assured herself. *She* certainly wasn't a loner. She liked being involved with everything and everyone. Dinah chose to be alone. She wanted to be left out of activities like the Spectacular. Katie didn't want that at all. And yet here she was—alone, just like Dinah.

It wasn't right. It wasn't fair. When the Spectacular was over, would everything be just as it was before? Or would she still be like Dinah—left out, excluded? The thought gave her a chill. But meanwhile, what was she going to do?

Her eyes scanned the cabin. The cabin five girls were busy with their quilting. In one corner, a bunch of the youngest campers were finger painting. At another table, Donna, the arts and crafts counselor, was showing a group how to knit. Nothing appealed to Katie.

She felt very odd, standing there alone in the room. Donna looked up and saw her. Any minute now, Katie knew she'd come tell her to join one of the groups.

From the back room, sounds of familiar chatter and laughter drifted out. And she couldn't stand it any longer. She absolutely had to see what they were up to.

Cautiously, she approached the door, edging herself against the wall, and peeked in. She could see Megan and Sarah applying wet paper towels to a huge mound. She knew that must be the rock the girls would have to move to rescue the spirit.

Erin was carefully glueing sequins to a crown. And Trina was painting dark green leaves on the forest scene that would serve as the background.

Watching her, Katie had to agree that a forest was probably the best background for the play. But the muddy brown and dark green looked awfully drab.

Just then, Trina turned around. Katie moved back from the door, but she wasn't quick enough. Trina had seen her. "Hi, Katie," she called out.

The others all turned then. And the room fell silent. Katie felt like an intruder. "Hi," she muttered.

Trina gestured toward the forest scene. "What do you think of this? Is it okay?"

Katie's eyes narrowed. What was she asking *her* for? They'd made it very clear they didn't want her opinion on anything.

She was aware that everyone was watching

93

her nervously. Was this a test or something? she wondered. They were probably expecting her to say something like, "It stinks." Maybe she was supposed to say, "It's fine, it's perfect," to show that she wanted to be involved in the play again.

"It's okay . . . I guess."

"No, really," Trina said insistently. "See, I think maybe it looks a little boring. And I can't think of any way to make a bunch of trees more interesting. C'mon, Katie, you always have ideas."

Katie's eyebrows shot up. What was going on here? Just the day before, they'd all made it very clear they didn't want her ideas.

But Trina must really want her opinion. She wasn't the type to play games. So Katie examined the scenery carefully.

"Why don't you put some fruit on the trees to add color?"

Erin considered this. "Yeah, that might work . . ."

Still looking at the scenery, Katie's idea grew. "And since the play is a fantasy, you wouldn't have to make the fruit ordinary red apples. The fruit could be silver and gold, maybe even glitter!" As she spoke, she could visualize the scene, and she started to get excited.

Then she caught herself. What was she doing? She wasn't a part of this anymore. Besides, all they would do is start arguing with her now. "I gotta go," she said abruptly. And she turned away and left the cabin. The only problem was, she had nowhere to go.

Somehow, Katie got through the afternoon. Luckily, cabin six had horseback riding, something she could do by herself. And rest period was okay, because everyone had to be quiet anyway.

But then, when rest period was over, came the time she'd been dreading—free period, when everyone else would be working on the play. While the others busied themselves getting ready, Katie pretended to be asleep, her eyes tightly shut. She didn't open them until she heard everyone leave and the cabin was silent.

But everyone hadn't left. Carolyn was still there, and she was standing by Katie's bunk. "Do you want to come to rehearsal with us, Katie?"

And do what? Katie asked silently. Watch while you do my job? She gave an exaggerated yawn. "No thanks. I think I'll just hang around here."

She could tell that Carolyn wanted to say something else. But she didn't. She just smiled gently, nodded, and left.

Katie watched from the window until they

were all out of sight. Then she climbed down from her bed. Dismally, she looked around the empty cabin. She didn't want to stay there alone. She went outside and started walking aimlessly. She didn't want to go near the dining hall, where the rehearsal was going on. And she avoided the activities building too—she really didn't want to run into other kids practicing their Spectacular acts. She decided to head over to the lakefront, where she could sit on a rock, look out at the water, and generally feel sorry for herself.

But just as she was passing the arts and crafts cabin, there was a loud crack of thunder. That was the only warning she got before the skies opened and rain poured down.

Katie ducked into the cabin. Since it was free period, there were several others inside working on projects of their own. They were all intent on their work, and no one noticed Katie.

Katie glanced toward the back room. She didn't hear any noise coming from there, and the room looked dark. They must all be over at the dining hall, she thought.

She knew she shouldn't care, but she couldn't help herself. She was dying for another look at the scenery. She wanted to see what they'd done to the boring trees. No one was there, so no one would have to know she still cared.

She slipped into the room, and turned on the light. Her eyes widened as she took in the sight that greeted her.

All over the green leafy trees, silver and gold apples had been painted on. Bits of glitter here and there made them sparkle. It was exactly what she'd told them to do, and it looked wonderful, just like she knew it would.

She heard footsteps behind her, and then a voice. "It looks nice, doesn't it?"

She whirled around. Trina and Sarah were standing there. Trina looked serious as she waited for a response to her question. Mutely, Katie nodded.

Sarah stepped forward and examined the scenery closely. "It's beautiful! It's got a real magical look. Thanks, Trina. You did a great job."

"It looked boring before. It was Katie's idea to add the gold and silver fruit."

"It was a good idea," Sarah said.

"Gee, thanks." Katie let plenty of sarcasm drip with those words. Sarah looked at her in surprise.

"You always have good ideas."

"Oh, yeah? How come you didn't think so before? Everytime I told you guys my ideas at rehearsal, everyone complained or argued with me."

Sarah and Trina looked at each other, as if

they were trying to decide what to say, and who should say it. "Katie," Sarah said, "we did like your ideas. But you expected too much! Yelling at us, telling all the kids they were lazy—"

"I was doing it for you!" Katie interrupted. "For all of us! I just wanted the play to be the best event at Spectacular! Isn't that what you want?"

"Not really," Sarah said. "I want it to be good. But it's not a contest, Katie."

"And you forgot about something," Trina added. "Spectacular is supposed to be fun." She paused, and then forced the next words out. "You were taking all the fun out of it."

Katie was about to object, but she realized she couldn't. Now that she thought about it, she realized Trina was right. It hadn't been much fun so far.

"Remember how much fun we had last year?" Sarah asked.

"Yeah," Katie said, "but the audience laughed at our performance."

Sarah shrugged. "So what? As long as we have a good time, who cares? Think back, Katie. The audience laughed at just about everyone. Except the ballet dancer, of course. But she was like a professional. We're not."

Katie sighed. Trina had said the same thing,

but she hadn't listened. "I was trying to be a good director."

"But you weren't being a director," Trina said gently. "You were being a boss. And nobody likes to get bossed around." She took a deep breath. "People have feelings, Katie. And you treated them like they didn't. I know you want the play to be a hit. But is that worth hurting people?"

The memory of Megan's stricken face crossed her mind. And she knew the answer to Trina's question.

"I should have listened to Carolyn," she murmured.

"What did she say?" Sarah asked.

"Something about how you catch more flies with honey than vinegar. Now I know what she means." She shook her head sadly. "I should have been nicer."

Trina cocked her head to one side thoughtfully, and then she smiled. "Katie . . . you still can be."

# Chapter 8

As quietly as possible, Katie slipped into the dining hall and stood by the door. Carolyn was onstage with the actors, and she was placing a chair down. "This is the cave opening, where the big rock will be, okay?" She came down from the stage, and the girls began. Fran, Becky, Megan, and Jill stood on one side of the chair. On the other side, Erin stood very still, her hands behind her back as if they were tied together.

Katie recognized the action on the stage. It was the scene where the girls were attempting to rescue the Spirit of Happiness. Since they were under the influence of the Spirit of Meanness, they couldn't get along at all.

" 'She must be behind that rock,' " Fran said.

" 'Oh, yeah?' " Jill asked in a nasty voice. " 'What makes you so sure of that?' "

" 'Because we've looked everywhere else, dummy,' " Fran snapped back at her.

" 'I think she's on top of that mountain,' " Megan announced, pointing off in the distance.

" 'That's impossible,' " Becky replied in a snotty voice. " 'The mountain's too steep for anyone to climb, even a spirit. You're just too stupid to know that.' "

" 'Hah!' " yelled Jill. " 'You're just too lazy to try climbing it.' "

" 'We have to get behind this rock,' " Becky said. " 'But how?' "

" 'I think we should climb over it,' " Jill said.

" 'No, it's too slippery,' " Fran said. " 'I know! We could move the rock!' "

" 'No!' " said Megan. " 'I think we should climb it!' "

" 'Move it!' " Becky yelled.

" 'Climb it!' " Jill shouted.

Jill and Megan pretended to try to climb the rock, raising their arms and then dropping them. Meanwhile Becky and Fran acted like they were trying to push the rock but couldn't.

" 'It's too slippery to climb!' " Jill said.

" 'It's too heavy to move!' " Becky cried out.

"Wait a minute," Carolyn called. She approached the stage. "This doesn't look right."

"Why not?" Megan asked.

"That's the problem," Carolyn said. "I'm not

**101**

sure. It's just that I don't think the audience will be able to see what you're doing, because of the way you're standing. Becky, you and Fran are blocking Megan and Jill. And I can't figure out how to position each of you so you're all visible. Do you guys have any ideas?"

They didn't. But Katie did. She could see the scene in her mind just the way it should look.

She took a deep breath. Then she came forward, her eyes lowered so she wouldn't have to see any hostile looks from the stage. "Carolyn?"

The counselor turned. "Hi, Katie. I didn't know you were here."

"I was watching from the back. I—I think I know how to fix the scene."

"Then tell me!" Carolyn said. "I'm desperate!"

Katie spoke softly so the girls on the stage couldn't hear. "Well, Megan and Jill could stay where they are. But Becky and Fran could be on the other side of the rock, with their backs to the audience. Then no one would be blocking anyone, and the audience could see what they're all trying to do." She paused. "What do you think of that?"

Carolyn considered it. "I think it just might work. Let's give it a try." She went forward and passed the directions on to the actors. They changed positions. And now the scene looked much better.

"Can we take a break?" Erin whined. "I'm getting sick of just standing here like this."

Katie had an instinctive urge to yell "too bad" at her. But she managed to restrain herself.

Carolyn responded. "I know it's tiring, Erin. But you'll have to get used to it, since this is what you'll be doing during the play. It's not that much longer." Her voice was firm, but soothing. Erin sighed, but nodded. And Katie realized she was getting a good example of the best way to catch flies.

Something else occurred to Katie. "Carolyn," she whispered, "to show that the rock is too heavy, shouldn't Fran and Becky be moaning or something?"

Carolyn nodded. "Good point." She passed the instructions on. Immediately, Fran and Becky started moaning and groaning. And even with just a little chair up there, Katie really got a feeling they were trying to move a huge rock.

"Katie," Carolyn said suddenly, "I have to run out for a minute. Could you take over?" Without waiting for a response, she handed the script to Katie and left.

Onstage, all action stopped. The actors just stood there, staring down at Katie.

Katie smiled nervously. "You can go on," she said.

The scene continued. " 'We can't budge this rock,' " Fran said.

" 'We can't climb it!' " Jill exclaimed.

" 'Oh no!' " Megan wailed. " 'It's impossible! We'll never be able to free the Spirit of Happiness!' "

From the other side of the chair-rock, Erin spoke loudly. " 'It is the mean feeling inside of you that prevents you from accomplishing this task. You must join together! Only with cooperation can you ever rescue me.' "

There was something wrong with the way she said that. Katie hesitated for a second. Then she said, "Erin?"

"What?"

"You sound so angry. I don't think a Spirit of Happiness would ever sound angry, do you?"

"No, I guess not. Maybe I should do it like this." She said her lines again, this time making the words sound more pleading.

"Perfect!" Katie said. For a second, Erin looked taken aback. The others did too. And Katie couldn't blame them. She'd probably never given any of them a compliment before.

The scene continued. The influence of the spirit caused all four to work together pushing the rock away, and the spirit was rescued.

It should have been the most thrilling moment of the play. But with the girls just standing there, smiling at Erin, it wasn't exactly exciting.

Katie knew what the scene needed. "What do you guys think of this? What if you all join hands and dance around her?"

She could have just ordered them all to do it. But saying it this way got a very different response than she'd gotten before as director.

"Yeah, that sounds good," Jill said. "Let's try it."

They did, and the little dance added just the right feeling of celebration. As Katie watched her idea in action, a thrill of pleasure swept through her.

From the other side of the stage, Jenny emerged. " 'Curses! How could her happiness triumph over my meanness?' "

Caught up in the play, Katie was barely aware of someone by her side. Then her heart sank. It was Carolyn. She didn't even know how long she'd been standing there.

Reluctantly, Katie held out the script to her. But Carolyn shook her head.

"I've been watching you from the back of the room. You don't need me. I think you can handle this fine on your own." She looked up at the actors. "Is it okay with you guys if Katie takes over?"

There was a general exchange of looks. Then came a chorus of "okays," and they were the sweetest okays Katie had ever heard.

"Thanks," Katie said humbly. "Now, let's get back to work."

# Chapter 9

It was the night of the Spectacular. The girls were gathered in cabin five next door, and Katie could feel the tension in the air. Or maybe it was just the tension inside of her.

But Megan's quivering voice made it clear the feelings were shared. "What if I forget my lines?"

Just a short time ago, Katie knew she would have responded with something like, "You better not!" But she'd learned a lot in the past week. And what she learned made her say instead, "Don't worry, Megan, you won't. But if you do, just look toward us offstage, and Sarah will whisper them to you."

"Props and scenery are all in the dining hall kitchen," Trina reported.

"And the costumes are there, too," Karen added.

"Where are we on the program?" Erin asked.

"We're last," Katie announced. This was greeted by loud groans. "No, no, that's good!" Katie told them. "People always remember the last act. Now, is there anything we've forgotten?"

There was a moment of silence as they pondered this. "What about makeup?" Becky asked.

"Makeup?" Katie turned to Carolyn. "Do we need makeup?"

"It's a good idea," Carolyn told her. "You'll look pale under the stage lights. And makeup on the two spirits would make them look more dramatic."

"I've got tons of makeup," Erin said. "I'll put everyone's on."

Katie was doubtful. "Thanks, Erin. But you might be too nervous. Does anyone else know how to put makeup on people?" She figured they could always use Carolyn as a last resort, but in the Spectacular tradition, she hoped to keep only campers involved.

From the back of the cabin, a voice spoke. "I know how to do stage makeup."

Everyone turned and looked at Dinah. Katie had forgotten she was even there. "Really?" she asked in delight.

"I *told* you, I've had professional theater lessons. And we learned how to do makeup."

"Would you do it for us tonight?" Katie asked.

Dinah shrugged. "I suppose I could. I don't have anything better to do." It wasn't a very gracious response, but Katie beamed at her anyway. Then she checked her watch. "It's time to go over there."

A nervous hush fell over the group. "Break a leg," Laura called out to them.

Katie looked at her in horror. "What?!"

Carolyn grinned. "It's a show-biz expression. It's bad luck to say good luck. You say, 'Break a leg,' instead."

It sounded totally confusing to Katie. She didn't have time to figure out what it meant now. But as the girls passed her to go outside, she whispered, "Don't break anything, okay?"

In front of the dining hall were buses from other camps in the area. Kids were getting off the buses and counselors were leading them in. The girls from cabins five and six headed directly to the kitchen area, but Katie couldn't resist a peek inside the main room.

The dining hall had been transformed. All the tables had been removed. Chairs had been set up in rows. And the chairs were rapidly filling up.

The scene in the kitchen and storage areas

was total chaos. Hordes of campers had gathered there to prepare for their shows. Ms. Winkle, the camp director, bustled through the crowd looking even more harried than usual. "You can't all be back here now! Only the first three acts! The rest of you go out and sit in the audience. Come back here when the act before yours goes on."

Katie was actually glad to hear this. At least watching the other shows should distract her group and keep them from getting too nervous. Feeling like a shepherd, she gathered her flock and led them back out to the main room.

She eyed the assembly with satisfaction. It looked like it was going to be a full house. Megan clutched Katie's arm. "There's—there's so many people! I can't act in front of all these people! They're scary!"

The little redhead had gone very pale. Katie patted her arm. "Just imagine that they're all in their underwear."

"In their underwear? Why?"

Katie grinned. "How scary can they be in their underwear?"

The whole gang found seats in the last two rows. The lights dimmed. Then Ms. Winkle came out on the stage in front of the closed curtain. "Good evening, and welcome to the Camp Sunnyside Spectacular. This is our annual variety show, where our campers show their talents. We hope you enjoy their performances."

Katie settled back and tried to put thoughts of the play out of her head. It wasn't easy. The first act was pretty boring. A bunch of the youngest campers came out, stood stiffly in a line across the stage, and one by one recited original poems each had written. Around the room, Katie could see people shifting restlessly in their seats. At least they didn't boo.

The next act got more attention. The girl who had done a ballet dance last year did another one. She was even better than she'd been before. The audience responded enthusiastically, and Katie was thankful they weren't coming on after her.

After that came cabin nine's fashion show. Each girl paraded around the stage in some fancy outfit while a narrator described it. The audience got restless again, and Katie could hear rumblings of conversation.

But the talking stopped when cabin seven came on with their rock show. The girls did their impersonations really well, with great makeup and costumes. They had the whole audience clapping and stamping their feet in time with the music.

There was a folk dance performance, a medley of patriotic songs, and two tap dancers. Finally it was time for Katie's group to go backstage and get ready.

Everyone was unusually quiet. Erin, who was normally so cool and confident, was shaking so much she couldn't even get her costume on. Trina had to help her get dressed, while Dinah worked on Jenny's makeup.

"How do I look?" Erin asked. For once, she didn't ask that with her usual I-know-I-look-gorgeous attitude. She actually sounded anxious.

"Wow!" Megan exclaimed. "Erin, you look beautiful!"

Katie had to agree. In the pale blue glittery gown, with the little crown on her head and the wand in her hand, she did look like someone special.

"I'm finished with Jenny," Dinah announced. She didn't ask what anyone thought of her work, but she didn't need to. The oohs and ahhs made everyone's opinion clear. Dinah had made Jenny look positively evil, with white makeup and black eyeliner extending way out beyond her eyes.

"Geez, Jenny, you don't even look like me!" Jill gasped.

"Dinah, you did a wonderful job," Katie said, hoping the compliment might make the sulky girl feel good. But Dinah was unimpressed. "I'll do Erin now."

"I want pale blue eye shadow," Erin said as she sat down in a chair by Dinah.

"I'll do what I think is best," Dinah said coldly. "And if you don't like it, you can do it yourself."

Katie shook her head in resignation. Dinah just didn't care if people liked her or not. Katie wondered if she'd ever know what she was missing.

Finally, they were all ready. Karen and Trina rushed to get the forest scene and the papier-mâché rock on the stage as the curtain from the previous act went down. And Katie gave the actors a quick pep talk. The only kind of pep talk she'd ever heard before was the one her soccer coach at school gave them right before every game. But she figured it would work just as well here.

"You've all worked really hard, and you're a great team. So go on out there and knock 'em dead!"

She wasn't sure if any of them had heard her. They were all looking pretty dazed as they followed Sarah around to the back of the stage. Katie came up from behind.

They could hear Ms. Winkle making the introduction. "Our next show is an original play called 'The Battle of the Spirits,' written by Sarah Fine and performed by campers from cabins five and six."

"Take your places," Katie hissed. Megan, Jill, Fran, Becky, and Erin ran out onto the stage. Jenny stood at the edge to wait for her entrance. The curtain went up, and the play began.

Katie had heard the lines a hundred times. But as she watched from backstage, it all sounded fresh and new. No one forgot a line, not even Megan. Erin was beautiful and charming. Jenny was frightening and dangerous. It was exciting, dramatic, and there wasn't a dull moment.

She peeked out at the audience. They were silent, and they all seemed totally caught up in the fantasy.

The story flew by, and it seemed like only seconds later when Erin was making her final speech.

" 'You see, although I was captured, I never really left you. For the Spirit of Happiness is always within you. But you must seek her out and keep her in your thoughts. When the Spirit of Meanness enters you, you must fight it off. Remember—if you love each other, if you care about each other, if you always work together, you'll never lose me.' "

Funny—Katie had read this speech and heard it, over and over. But for the first time, she knew what the words really meant.

And then it was over. The curtain came down. And the audience burst into applause. It wasn't a standing ovation—but it was definitely loud.

The curtain came back up, and the actors took their bows. Out in the audience, someone—sounding very much like Carolyn—cried out, "Author, author!"

Sarah seemed frozen. Katie had to practically push her out onstage. Sarah stiffly bowed. The applause continued. And then, from the stage, came a rhythmic chant from the actors. "Director! Director! Director!"

Now it was Katie's turn to freeze. And it took both Karen and Trina to shove her out on the stage.

Katie stood there, unable to even bow. Dimly, she realized the applause was coming from behind her, as well as in front of her. It dawned on her that the audience looked awfully blurry. And she realized that was because of the tears in her eyes.

The applause was dying down, but no one onstage cared. They joined hands across the stage and took one more bow as the curtain came down. And if there really was something like a

Spirit of Happiness in the world, Katie knew she was with them, right that minute. And she made a silent vow to keep that spirit within herself from now on.

# MEET THE GIRLS FROM CABIN SIX IN

### CAMP SUNNYSIDE #8
### TOO MANY COUNSELORS
75913-6 ($2.95 US/$3.50 Can)

In only a week, the Cabin Six girls go through three counselors and turn their cabin into a disaster zone. Somehow camp without their regular counselor, Carolyn, isn't as much fun as they thought it would be.

*Don't Miss These Other*
*Camp Sunnyside Adventures:*

| | |
|---|---|
| **(#7) A WITCH IN CABIN SIX** | 75912-8 ($2.95 US/$3.50 Can) |
| **(#6) KATIE STEALS THE SHOW** | 75910-1 ($2.95 US/$3.50 Can) |
| **(#5) LOOKING FOR TROUBLE** | 75909-8 ($2.50 US/$2.95 Can) |
| **(#4) NEW GIRL IN CABIN SIX** | 75703-6 ($2.50 US/$2.95 Can) |
| **(#3) COLOR WAR!** | 75702-8 ($2.50 US/$2.95 Can) |
| **(#2) CABIN SIX PLAYS CUPID** | 75701-X ($2.50 US/$2.95 Can) |
| **(#1) NO BOYS ALLOWED!** | 75700-1 ($2.50 US/$2.95 Can) |
| **MY CAMP MEMORY BOOK** | 76081-9 ($5.95 US/$7.95 Can) |